TIMBERLINE TRAIL

ROCKY MOUNTAIN SAINT BOOK 5

B.N. RUNDELL

WOLFPACK
PUBLISHING
— EST 2013 —

Timberline Trail
(Rocky Mountain Saint Book 5)
B.N. Rundell

Paperback Edition
© Copyright 2018 B.N. Rundell

Wolfpack Publishing
6032 Wheat Penny Avenue
Las Vegas, NV 89122

ISBN: 978-1-64119-376-4

Readin', Ritein', an' Rithmetic. Also known as the three R's of early education. I attended a one-room country school house (still standing!) in Howard, Colorado. Three of my older brothers were in the same school as one teacher, Mrs. Ellsworth, taught eight grades the three R's. I often think back to those times, walking the hillside trail to school, the two outhouses out back, the water jug with a spigot, and the old wooden desks, all connected, and each with its own inkwell. It was then I learned the adventures of reading and began to develop the dream of writing. Now, the Lord has blessed, and I've been able to write seventeen novels, (this is the 17th) and will continue writing, that is as long as there are willing readers. For without readers, I wouldn't have the opportunity to write. Thank you to so many! I'm thankful for readers, and those that go a little bit further to encourage me with your reviews, and especially to all of you that recommend my books to others. You're the greatest! And a special thank you to my ever-patient wife who listens as I read each chapter to her for her review and recommendations! The 'new' three R's. Thanks Babe, you're my favorite!

TIMBERLINE TRAIL

CHAPTER ONE
MESSAGE

"You know how I've always talked about exploring the Rockies, even when we sat at the table and talked about our future. I guess I'm just getting restless, I don't really want to leave you, but, what should I do? It's been so long." Tate Saint sat on the big log he had carved into a bench, elbows on knees and hands clasped. His hat sat on the bench beside him and the sun shone bright in a clear blue sky, casting his shadow on the grave of his beloved wife, White Fawn. Lobo, the big grey wolf lay on his belly beside the bench, head resting between his paws as he waited for the man who was his friend and partner. Tate looked through the break in the pines to the lake that nestled in the valley below. The corner of his cabin showed just beyond the line of ponderosa that sheltered the clearing where the mound with spring wild-flowers lay.

"I guess I'm still lost without you. When I came west, it was to see the mountains and make a life here. We did that for a while, but you remember me tellin' you about that first cabin I built, down in the Sangre de Cristos. I was kinda thinkin' 'bout goin' down there for a spell. Oh, I'd come back here, you know that, don't you?" There was no answer coming from the mound below the hand carved cross that read "White Fawn, beloved wife of Tate Saint." His eyes roved over the clusters of spring flowers, the mountain bluebells, purple larkspur, a cluster of small white daisies, and several of the taller Golden Banner were blooming behind the cross. Nearer the trees by the small spring, a sizable chokecherry bush showed its white blossoms. White Fawn loved all the flowers in the mountains, but her favorites were the many different columbines, but they wouldn't show color for at least another month.

Of all the places he had been, this mountain hideaway had the most beautiful setting of all. The cabin was tucked back into the trees but afforded a view of the lake below and the mountains beyond. The southern end of the Wind River Mountains held this isolated getaway and Tate would always love this place and would never surrender his refuge. But the wanderlust was upon him and he knew he would be on the trail somewhere, but he wasn't sure where or when.

"Hello the cabin!" called a raspy voice from below the clearing, and hidden in the trees. Tate jumped to his feet and in the same motion lifted his Hawken before him, a quick glance reassured him of the cap on the nipple showing the rifle was ready for use.

He answered, "Yo, who are you and whatdoya want?" As he spoke he moved slowly down the slope, holding near the trees for cover if needed.

"This is Bridger! If you're the kid that's friends with Carson, I gotta message!"

"I'm comin' down!" answered Tate as he picked up his pace.

The mountain man was easily recognizable, with what

some had called 'beady eyes' that made him appear as if he was squinting at the sun all the time. Tate greeted him with, "A message? Who'd be sendin' me a message?"

"Carson, that's who. I was down at Bent's Fort when I run into the ol' coot and when I tol' him I was comin' up this-away, he asked me to give you the message," explained the mountain man.

"Well, what's the message?"

"He said for you to come down to Bent's place cuz he's got a job fer you!"

"A job? I don't need no job. What kinda job, did he say?" asked Tate, scowling.

"Nope, just said you need to skedaddle on down there, cuz he'd be a waitin' fer you. So, you gonna make me stand 'roundchere all day, or you gonna fix some coffee?" asked Bridger.

"Oh, oh, sure, c'mon in. I'll put some coffee on. Sorry 'bout that. I ain't seen or talked to nobody since last summer. Guess I plum forgot muh manners," explained Tate as he mounted the steps to the cabin.

Coffee cups steaming with the fresh black brew, the men were seated at the table when Tate asked, "So, what brings you up thisaway? You ain't gonna be trappin' are ya?"

"No, no, not trappin'. What with the market 'most gone fer beaver, an' too many trappers turnin' to peltries of other kinds, 'specially buffler, no, I turned the comp'ny over to muh partners. I'm thinkin' 'bout puttin' in a fort to sell to all them settlers movin' through. They'll be needin' supplies and fixin's. I'm thinkin' 'bout down on the Green, south a ways."

"Logical, logical, I reckon. I know them settlers I was with last summer coulda used some resupply by the time they got up on South Pass. I guess they made it the rest o' the way alright, don't know for sure. Hope so," Tate was staring into his coffee as he spoke, remembering the wagon train of farmers he guided from Fort William to the pass.

"Well, if'n you don't get too busy with Carson, an' you come back thisaway, look us up. Might be able to find you some work," suggested the noted frontiersman.

"Now, what'd I do that makes all you old timers think I need to go to work? Can't you stand the thought of somebody that's happy just bein' in the mountains and not workin' for somebody?"

"Wal, ever'body needs some money, ever' now n' then, just cuz. Don'tchu?" asked Bridger.

"If you can't eat it, and it don't keep you warm, what do I want with it?" pleaded Tate.

Bridger grinned at the man, who was about half his age, and said, "I've worked as a trapper, guide, soldier, scout, and many other things. Learned a lot, too. Even owned muh own company, the Rocky Mountain Fur Company. Probably gonna go together with ol' Louie Vasquez an' build a tradin' fort. And, believe you me, I've always had use for money."

"Wal, mebbe when I get old, like you an' Carson, I'll be needin' money for my old age, but for now, I'm fine."

"Why you young whippersnapper! If Carson had tol' me what a smart-alec you were, I'd have tol' him to bring his own message! Old, don't you go usin' that word about me, I'll have to take yore britches down an' give you whut for!" blustered the mountain man, draining his coffee cup with a big gulp and holding it out for more.

"So, how long's it gonna take me to get to Bent's Fort?" asked Tate, sipping his fresh cup of java.

"Well, I made it in a day more'n three weeks. But for a greenhorn like you, it might take you all of a month or two!" bantered Bridger, poking fun at what he considered a youngster.

"Wal, guess you oughta spend the night, an' make sure I pack right for such a long trip. Ya reckon?" jibed Tate.

Bridger made a show of looking around the cabin and said, "You'll prob'ly need to pack ever'thing. I'd hate for you to have it too rough on the trail, bein' so young an' all."

CHAPTER TWO
SOUTHWEST

BRIDGER DIDN'T SPEND THE NIGHT, HE TOLD TATE HIS PARTY was waiting for him atop South Pass and he had business to attend to and with a hasty goodbye, the mountain man made his getaway. Tate began gathering his gear together as the dusk began giving way to darkness, but the packing of the parfleches and the packs would be done by firelight. He was excited about the message from Carson, after all, he had just spoken about his lack of direction and now that had been decided. It would be good to see his friend and mentor, even though he had no idea nor interest in this 'job' he spoke of, but at least it got him moving.

He checked his gear and supplies, reassuring himself he had everything he needed. Yet once done, he stood with hands on his hips, then scratching his head he asked Lobo, "So, what'm I forgettin' boy?" Lobo got up from his corner and walked to the packs, sniffing and looking, then looked up at Tate as if to say, "What're you askin' me for?"

"Well, that's all I can think of, so how 'bout we try to get some sleep. We'll be leavin' purty early." Tate turned to bank the fire in the fireplace, push his packs against the far wall, and went to his bed, Lobo trailing behind. When dark came in the mountains, the temperature would plummet, even in the early spring. The dark shadows of the thick pines harbored many snowdrifts that stubbornly resisted the increasing warmth and would until well into the summer. And the cool nights were good for sleeping nestled under the thick pile of buffalo robes and blankets. He tried to sleep, but Tate tossed and turned, kicked off the blankets, and sat on the edge of his bed looking down at Lobo. He guessed it was well past midnight and got up to put on a pot of coffee. He did a cursory check of his gear, trying to think of anything he needed that wasn't packed, and shook his head as he returned to the fire to heat up the last of the cornbread and fried pork belly from the night before. He tossed some of the meat to Lobo and sat at the table, looking at his breakfast as he began to pray.

It was his habit to start every day in prayer, a habit learned as a youngster at home with his folks in the hills of Missouri. His Pa was a schoolteacher and his Ma a self-taught nurse and midwife and both were devout Christians. While Pa kept him in books, Ma kept him in the Bible and he was thankful for both. His coming to the mountains was the fulfillment of a life-long dream he shared with his Pa and after he lost both his parents, he came west in pursuit of that dream.

Now at the ripe old age of twenty-one, he was considered a seasoned mountain man and even an old-timer by some standards. Known as Longbow by many different bands of natives because of his proficiency with his English style w and his many encounters and resulting friendships, he was becoming known as the Rocky Mountain Saint by others. His given name was Tatum St. Michael, but that had been shortened to Tate Saint long ago. His purpose for coming to the mountains was to have a solitary life, free from restrictions and demands of civilization and other people-made problems, but somehow, he always found himself involved in others lives and their problems.

Because of his discovery of an old Spanish mine and stash of gold bars in the Sangre de Cristo mountains, and his subsequent deposit of that gold in a St. Louis bank, keeping a considerable amount in gold coin, he was a wealthy man. But that was something he kept close to his chest and shared with no one. While other mountain men had to trap beaver or take other peltries to trade for their supplies, the few times Tate had to re-supply with gear and staples, it was handy to have the gold. He had fashioned many places to stash the coin, like in the pommel of his saddle, the lining of the saddle bags, the end of his rifle scabbard and others. He felt those pockets to reassure himself all was safe and sat back in the chair when he finished.

He stepped out on his porch and from the steps, he looked up at the star-filled sky. A quick recognition of several constellations brought a smile to his face as his eyes lingered on the Hunter, or Orion, and the times he and White Fawn, his Arapaho bride, had sat under the stars and he told her about the names he learned, and she told him the native names of some of the same constellations. The Hunter was their favorite and he would often point it out whenever they were out at night. The moon was resting atop the pines on the western horizon as Tate walked to the grave to say his goodbye.

It was mid-morning when Tate, aboard Shady, the blue-grey grulla gelding, and leading the long-legged blaze faced black as his pack horse, rode into the clearing at the top of South Pass. He stood in his stirrups and looked about, enjoying the warm sun from the cloudless blue sky, and searched the flats and the trail east and west. It had been some time since he had been on the flats, last summer to be exact, and it was good to feel the wide-open spaces again. He pointed Shady to the south, choosing to take his own path rather than the wider trail that was gradually becoming a well-used wagon road of the Oregon Trail.

They moved through a sparse cluster of pines, dropped off the shoulder of the flat-top plateau and started down the rocky slope toward Slaughterhouse gulch. Tate knew this would lead to the headwaters of the Sweetwater River and he would follow that river a short distance before cutting across to the southeast toward the distant mountains. With a wave of his hand he sent Lobo ahead to scout their trail and Shady pricked his ears forward to watch his friend trot off. Tate used the dim light of dusk to find a campsite among the willows on the banks of the winding Sweetwater. Cover was non-existent, but the grass was abundant and fresh water handy, so the camp would be a pleasant and beneficial one, at least for the animals.

Bridger had warned him, "Now, crossin' them flats from the Sweetwater to the Sierra Madre is gonna be hot an' dry. So, be sure to water up an' cross them alkali flats in the cool of the day. Even this early in the season, it'll be hotter'n Hades out there." Because of that warning, Tate had determined to resort to his usual practice of traveling at night making full use of the available springtime moonlight. He knew the moon was waxing full and they would have ample time for the week-long crossing. With four hours of rest and grazing, he knew Shady and the black would be ready. As he swung aboard the grulla, he lifted his eyes to the broad star-studded sky, and with the North Star behind his left shoulder, he clucked the gelding on his way.

IT WAS early morning on the sixth day of travel when the alkali dusted group finally found a clear stream at the edge of the ponderosa, beneath the granite peak that marked the Sierra Madre mountain range. Tate wasted no time in finding a deep backwater pool and as quickly as he could, he dropped the packs and other gear and led the two horses into the still water to rid themselves of the dry powdery alkali dust that seemed to have infiltrated every pore of their skin. The horses dipped their heads under the water to wash out their nostrils and eyes, glad for the refreshing wetness. Tate sat down in the deep water, splashing around to rid himself of the choking powder, then he took off his buckskins, tossed them on the shore and did the same with his union suit. Lobo stood on the shore watching his companions and dropped his head between his feet and he jumped side to side, whining and growling. Finally giving in, he jumped in and swam toward Tate. The man grasped the wolf's head, rubbed noses with the beast, and splashed water on the thick ruff at the wolf's neck as the two cavorted about like kids.

Back on shore, he turned to call the horses from the water as Lobo stood beside him. With only his underdrawers on, the man was a laughable sight in the morning light, but the dripping water on his muscular chest and arms glistened in the sun, showing his the lean body of the man. Standing six feet tall with broad shoulders and tapered torso to a narrow waist, his dark brown hair hung to his shoulders. He would soon rid himself of the patchy whiskers that darkened his face beneath his hazel eyes. When the horses came from the water he slapped them on the rump toward the grassy clearing.

He hung the union suit on a chokecherry bush but donned his damp buckskins. Although Indian tanned and made, the smoked skins were water resistant but would dry softer and better if worn, and he didn't like being without his buckskins. A small fire sufficed for coffee and the handful of pemmican served for his breakfast. He looked to the sky to see a clear day ahead and the sweet smell of pine told him he was back in his element. Here he could relax and rest, with Lobo and the horses on guard, he was confident he could get some good sleep before starting the next, more mountainous, leg of his journey.

CHAPTER THREE
DISCOVERY

BACK IN MOUNTAINOUS COUNTRY, TATE OPTED FOR DAYTIME travel. "We ain't seen this country before Lobo, so, I'm all for takin' our time and enjoying the scenery. How 'bout'chu boy?" His habit of talking to the wolf accomplished little more than take the edge off the solitude. Although there were times he was almost certain the wolf understood everything he said, there were also times he knew Lobo just tolerated the talkative trail partner. With the mountains just to his west still holding considerable snow, he kept to a trail near the bottom of the wide valley, staying close to the treeline for ready cover. Well supplied with dried and smoked meat, he hadn't taken the time to do any hunting, but if something crossed his path that whetted his appetite, he would willingly take some fresh meat. For now, he just enjoyed the restless herds of elk that grazed on the fresh grasses but kept their eyes on the mountains and their summer range that beckoned. He never tired of watching the majestic animals, although at this time of year the big bulls had yet to grow back their massive antlers. Tate would occasionally mimic the grunts and calls of the elk, just to see them raise their heads and curiously search the surrounding terrain for the unusual visitor.

Late on the fourth day of mountain travel, Tate was looking for a camp site and had been eyeing the mountain slope to his right, having an inclination to do a little exploring. When he spotted what appeared as an opening to a canyon with walls of limestone, he pointed the grulla to follow the cascading stream that came from the gorge. The trees on the sides of the ravine gave way to grassy slopes the nearer he drew to the canyon. Tate looked to the wolf and said, "Lobo, looks like we're gonna get wet, cuz near as I can tell, there's a trail over there and the canyon walls come down right to the water over on this side. So, how 'bout you leadin' the way?" he motioned to the wolf to cross overand Lobo instantly responded, splashing water aside as he crossed the narrow creek. The water was fast, crashing over the rocks with white froth, but not very deep and within moments, Lobo stood waiting as the horses waded across.

The change of scenery was exhilarating as Tate searched the jagged cliffs and rocky hillsides for any sign of life. One of the reasons for taking this side trip was in hopes of spotting a bighorn sheep, thinking it would make for some good eating. He looked at the trail before him and found it a little curious. *If this was just a game trail, it wouldn't be so worn down and smooth, and not as wide either. This trail has been traveled by men on horseback. Now, what do you suppose is up this canyon that has men travelin' thisaway?* As his mind wandered with curious twists and turns, he watched his surroundings for any sign of life, man or beast.

The trail bent around an outthrust of the canyon wall and suddenly before him a lush valley stretched out and seemed to climb the mountainside as it turned to the fresh green that told of aspen. The cliff to his left pulled away to yield to the blend of fir, spruce and pine that seemed to march like a brigade of green uniformed soldiers up the steep mountain-side. Tate looked back at the jagged limestone cliff and saw an overhang that showed itself as a promising camp. He gigged his horses into the flat grassy area in front of the overhang and reined up, recognizing this as a site that had been used many times before by wilderness travelers. There was no sign of recent visits, but the blackened roof of the overhang told of previous campfires and a weathered grey pole that hung between two nearby trees told of hunting camps.

While he de-rigged his horses, he let his eyes continue to wander and search what he could see of the valley. Where he camped gave a great panoramic view of this entire hollow that nestled between the mountains and he had already seen plenty of fresh sign of game. He dropped the packs and saddle near the back wall of the overhang when something caught his eye on the cliff face to his left. As he drew near, he stopped and stared in wonder. Before him, from about shoulder level and about three or four feet higher, was an assortment of petroglyphs. These were not the first ancient pictures he had seen carved into the face of stone, but this grouping was the most impressive. The images before him showed a herd of what was undoubtedly elk with large antlers on many of the figures. Indian hunters with bows and arrows were seen as broad stick figures holding the bows as they aimed at the elk herd. Behind them was a village of tipis and other people. In another spot were hunters mounted on horses and chasing buffalo, recognizable by the humps and small horns.

As he examined the images before him he wondered, *Now, how'd they do that? And those pics are higher than I can reach, how'd they get that high? I'd like to know when that was done too, probably before white men came. There's no guns shown, just spears and bows. Hmm, ain't that sumpin'?*

He turned away from the cliff face and caught movement across the creek on the opposite hillside. Coming from the rock formations above and beside the canyon walls was a line of Bighorn sheep. They were led by a couple of ewes and pushed by a big ram with a massive set of horns that were more than a full curl. Other rams preceded the herd boss, but there were more ewes and lambs than rams. Tate had seen the procession through a cut in the treetops and he knew he and his horses were out of sight.

His first choice for hunting was usually his bow, not wanting to broadcast his presence with a rifle shot, but the sheep were wary animals and watchful. He doubted he would get close enough to use his bow effectively, so he opted for the Hawken. Withdrawing it from the scabbard, he placed a cap on the nipple, and with his powder horn and possibles bag already draped over his shoulders, he started a stealthy approach of the sheep. He hoped to meet them at the creek and take one after the others drank, but he couldn't be too choosy on his shot.

After the rest of the small herd had their drink, the rams pushed forward and with their front feet on the gravel by the bank, they stuck their noses in the water. Tate chose one of the younger rams, preferring to leave the older and probably tougher herd ram to watch his flock. The blast from the Hawken broke the silence of the valley and bounced from wall to wall as it echoed from the tree-lined creek bank. The light gray smoke pointed the way to the downed ram that had dropped the instant the .54 caliber ball found its mark. Tate waded the stream and began field dressing the animal, tossing scraps to the waiting Lobo. The hunter anticipated the fresh meat for his supper and planned on smoking the rest to replenish his supply.

WHEN MORNING'S light told Tate he had slept longer than usual, he quickly rolled from his blanket and started his morning routine to get back on the trail. But as he busied himself, he paused and thought, *I'm gonna explore this little valley a bit, just cuz. I'm thinkin' it might have more secrets to find.* He left his horses on the grass but took Lobo with him on his short trek. Leaving the Hawken and taking his longbow, he started climbing alongside the cliff face among the scattered rock formations. He had no sooner started across the rocky face when he spotted a formation that didn't appear quite natural. When he approached the cluster of boulders, he noticed the end of an aged aspen log protruding from the stack and he stopped in his tracks. *This is a burial! Carson said the Ute's burials were similar to the Comanche and they buried their people in the rocks, caves, and such.* He walked closer and saw a small scrap of beaded leather, probably brought from the cairn by a marmot or other rodent. Out of respect, he backed away and walked around, looking for other formations that would tell of burials. He remembered that many of the mountain tribes had the custom that when the man died, his personal possessions, especially his weapons of war would be buried with him. Also, his wife or wives would be put to death to join him on his journey to the other side, and sometimes any captives that had served as his slaves and at least his favorite horse or horses would also be put to death. All for the purpose of equipping the man for his journey. Tate stepped up on a large rocky outcropping of moss covered limestone and looked around the bowl-shaped valley. He saw three or four other sites that were probably burial cairns. *This is what my old friend, Knuckles, would call Cañón de los Muertos or the Canyon of the Dead,* thought Tate.

A strip of green that came from the face of the mountain and pointed to the valley floor drew Tate's attention, thinking it was probably a spring fed creek and a drink would be just what he wanted. Watching his step as he made his way across the slide rock on the face of the slope, he followed Lobo to the small stream and both man and beast immersed their faces in the ice-cold water. As he sat back up and wiped his face, a glimmer from the water caught his eye and he looked closer. The stream was no more than two or three feet wide with a depth of about four or five inches, but it ran crystal clear and showed every pebble. Tate looked at the assortment of quartz stones and other pebbles of a variety of colors, but what had caught his attention was color just at the bottom edge of a larger stone that protruded from the stream. He reached down and brought out a small handful of smooth stones, each about the size of his fingernail. Three of the five stones were solid gold nuggets.

"Oh great," he groaned at the realization of what he had found. He dropped to his rump on the rocks and looked around at the beautiful little valley. "That's all this place needs is a bunch of greedy miners diggin' for gold! Right in the middle of an Indian burial ground!" He reached down and rumpled the fur at Lobo's neck and added, "Well boy, let's get outta here! We don't need anybody findin' us here and startin' some kinda gold rush. Now, remember," he looked at Lobo sternly, "don't you go tellin' nobody about this place, understand?" The two followed the little stream to the valley bottom and trotted back to their camp. In just a short while, Tate looked over his shoulder at the canyon and said, "Cañón de los Muertos, keep your secrets!"

CHAPTER FOUR
REVELATION

THE CLOUDS WERE LYING LOW ON THE MOUNTAINS AND drifting down to the valley floor. Tate and company moved through the wispy white, Shady following the bushy tail of Lobo as he explored the trail before them. In his thoughts, Tate was still back in the canyon. He pictured the petroglyphs and the 'people that came before' as the natives referred to those that left their mark and remembrances or stories etched in stone. The image of the burial cairns stood out as the sentinels on the mountain side. As always, whenever he discovered anything new and different, he thought of his father and wondered what his reaction might have been.

Allowing Shady to have his head as he shuffled along the pine needle covered trail, Tate's eyes glassed over as he remembered. His father would often take a simple happening or new discovery and relate it to the stories in the Scriptures. As Tate thought about the canyon he could hear his father compare the petroglyphs to the events in the Old Testament. He would probably say, "Just like the old testament prophets, those that carved their stories in stone told how their people lived, and maybe, like Moses and the tablets of stone that were given by God, those pictures told of laws to live by. Now, those burial cairns, they had poles covered by stone, not unlike the rugged cross that bore our Savior, Jesus, and he was buried in a cave and it was covered with a big stone. Now, as to the gold, after one studies the Scriptures and learns of God, and comes to accept Jesus as their savior, he finds the water of life, Jesus, and untold riches in his life, not unlike the riches of gold in the clear water of the stream."

Tate smiled at the thought, almost hearing the voice of his father say those very words. And if his mother had heard, she would have smiled knowingly, nodding her head all the time in agreement. Tate had often remembered the times his family had spent at the table, after their meals, just sharing the events and discoveries of the day. He had often told of his wanderings in the woods with his Osage friend, Red Calf, and would frequently receive an admonition from his mother about being careful in the wilderness. If she could only see him now, thought Tate, grinning to himself.

When Bridger had visited his cabin, Tate kept the explorer and experienced mountain man up late, quizzing him and picking his mind of all the locations and landmarks in the Rockies to the south. He had followed the man's directions and was enjoying what he had termed the 'Scenic Route' through the mountains. After leaving the petroglyph canyon, their trail had taken them to the Colorado river, and Tate had followed the river from a flat-top plateau overlooking the canyon of the Colorado.

When the mountains opened up and left the canyon behind, Bridger's directions took them back into the mountains to the south. It was there he saw the landmark so vividly described by Bridger. He called it the "Mountain with a cross and a angel. It's formed by the snow that's held by them jagged rocks on the face o' that mountain. And at the foot o' that cross, the snow, if ya' look real careful, looks like a angel is kneelin' an' prayin' toward that there cross. Durnedest sight I ever saw in these hyar mountains, yessir."

Once Tate sighted the mountain, he reined up and stepped down for a better look. He took his father's spyglass from his saddle bags and stretched it out for a close-up view of such a wonder. He saw the black granite stone-face and the snow, still held in the crevices. It was on the north side and protected from the hot sun, keeping the snow almost as a glacier that stayed well into the warmer months. He lowered the telescope and looked, easily making out the forms described by the mountain man. His heavy sigh lifted his shoulders as he marveled at the handiwork of the Creator. His father had often said, "If we didn't have the Bible, God would tell us His story with creation itself."

"Now, you go upstream from that mountain wit' th' cross an' you'll cross oer' a pass and the water'll be runnin' th' other direction. Foller that down, oh, 'bout a day into a wide valley with a big ol' mountain range to the west. That's what some'er callin' the Sawatch Range. Now, you can either follow that river, that's the Arkansas, on down along them mountains, through a long narrow canyon an' it'll lead ya into the flats an' on to Bent's fort. Or, ya' can cut to the east o'er them smaller mountains and you'll break out into Bayou Salado, big ol' wide valley. You cut southeast 'crost it, an' you'll come back to the Arkansas. It's easier goin' thataaway, 'n ya' don't hafta fight them hills along the river canyon. If'n I was you, that's the way I'd go," explained Bridger, nursing the last of his coffee at Tate's table.

It was the end of his second week away from his cabin when he broke from the trees to see the panoramic vista of the Bayou Salado. He reined up on the bare hillside, stepped down and stretched his arms above his head as he twisted around to take in the vastness of the scene before him. The wide grassy valley of low rolling hills appeared barren at first. But as he sat on a wide flat rock, watched Lobo take off after a long-legged jackrabbit, and began taking in the view, he saw a fertile plain. Several streams carved their way across the flats, often stopped on their way with a series of beaver ponds. The usual aspen and spruce that bordered the streams had been felled by the flat-tailed rodents to make their mound homes in the midst of the ponds. The sun glistened across the surface of a pair of distant lakes, and the low rolling hills held to the pinyon and juniper that dotted their flanks. He lifted his spyglass to search the perimeter of the wide valley and saw several sizable herds of buffalo and antelope.

It took all of two days to cross Bayou Salado, but when they made the timber of the foothills on the southeast edge, Tate also had a pack full of fresh buffalo, some yet to be smoked. A small stream bordered by quakies beckoned with a grassy knoll in the shade for a camp for the night. The light breeze made the aspen whisper their welcome as Tate began to set up his smoking racks, cut from the thin white barked saplings of the grove. Lobo had caught the scent of his supper and took off through the trees in hot pursuit and Shady and the black were taking their drinks from the little stream. Soon the long thin strips of buffalo were soaking up the smoke from the alder wood Tate gathered earlier and he turned to prepare his supper.

When Lobo returned, there were a couple of small feathers caught in the corner of his lips and Tate saw, upon examination, they were from a prairie chicken. He remembered the first time he saw the wolf take a prairie chicken. The bird had held his place until Lobo was within about five feet, then instantly took flight, but Lobo's leap that took him at least six feet in the air, resulted in a feathery catch that he brought to earth and soon devoured. Tate rubbed his friend's scruffy neck and asked, "So, didja get your full? I hope so, cuz I ain't givin' you my steak!" Lobo didn't answer, nor did he get a steak.

Tate would usually have his supper, put out the fire and move his camp at least a mile or two away before bedding down for the night. But with the fresh meat smoking, Tate decided to stay and finish the task without moving his camp. It was just as dark was pushing the last color from the western sky, when Lobo let a low growl tell Tate of the approach of someone or something. Tate looked to the horses who also stood, ears up and looking toward the far edge of the stream. He swung a leg over the log he was sitting on, straddling it and slipping his Paterson Colt from the holster to hold it out of sight beside his leg. He motioned Lobo to the woods and he eared back the hammer as he listened to the footsteps approaching the camp.

"Hello the camp!" came a cry from the woods. The footsteps had stopped as whoever had called out waited for a reply. It was the practice of any woodsman to announce themselves before entering another's camp. Common sense said it was best to be expected and welcomed than shot on suspicion.

Tate answered, "Come ahead on, if you're friendly."

The footsteps began again, Tate recognizing there were at least two coming by the sounds. "Oh, we're friendly 'nuff, yessir. Smelled your coffee and hoped to get a cup, if'n ya' got 'nuff, that is."

Two men stepped from the trees, took a long leap across the stream and stood facing Tate. Both had rifles held across their chests, Tate noted neither rifle was cocked, and the men had pistols in their belts with powder horns and possibles bags on either side. Their buckskins were darkened by many meals that caused the men to wipe greasy hands on the skins to improve the water-shedding. These were experienced men of the woods, probably trappers or at least hide hunters.

The man at the front was the speaker for the pair, a little taller but lean. His mouth, what could be seen through the whiskers, smiled, but his eyes didn't. The other man, older and with a sprinkling of white in his beard, didn't bother to try to show friendliness. Both gave the camp a quick looking over, noting the horses and the packs and just one man before them. The talker said, "Well, we was just wantin' some coffee, but looks like you're purty well outfitted, it do. Is that buffler ya' got smokin' yonder?"

Tate nodded his head slowly, watching both men carefully, without answering.

The speaker looked at his partner and said, "He's a talkative one, ain't he Gus?"

"Ummhummm, shore is, Frankie," answered the oldster.

Tate watched as Gus slowly brought his thumb forward to start to ear back the hammer of his rifle at the same time Frankie started to lower the muzzle of his rifle and turn toward Tate. But before either action could be completed, Tate stood as he brought up the Paterson, and shot Frankie in the upper arm, knocking him back into Gus. The first man shouted as he was hit and stumbled back into his partner, causing them both to fall backwards into the stream. Tate stepped quickly to the stream bank as the two slapped at each other and the stream, trying to get their footing and he commanded, "Just sit still right where you're at!"

"What'd you shoot me fer?" demanded the talker.

"Well, ya know, I just couldn't see myself just sittin' there while the two of you shot me!"

"Let us git outta this water! It's colder'n a snowbank!" whined the older of the two.

"That's alright, you two just sit there. Hand me up your rifles, easy now. We both know your powder's wet and they ain't good for nothin' but clubs. So, one at a time." The disgruntled pair complied, mumbling their disgust all the while. Tate added, "Now, hand me those pistols and horns." Again, they complied. Tate holstered the Colt and with rifles and gear in hand, backed away from the stream and dropped the armload in a heap close to his packs.

"Hey! I'm bleedin' here! Let us git outta here!" demanded the one called Frankie.

"Alright, but take it easy now," answered Tate, now with his Colt held before him as he watched.

When they stood on the grassy bank, the two wiped the water from their buckskins and stood shivering in the light evening breeze that cut through the trees.

"Can we at least come to the fire?" whined Gus.

Tate motioned them over and had them sit cross-legged on the far side of the small fire. They stretched out their hands to the flickering flames and looked at their captor.

"Where's your horses?" asked Tate. He saw the quick glance from one to the other and knew whatever they answered would be a lie, but he waited for their response.

"Injuns took 'em. We been afoot for three days now, that's why we come to your camp. Them Injuns took everything!" growled Frankie.

Tate knew that if the Indians had taken everything, they would have also taken the men's rifles and scalps, yet here they were, unharmed and with all their hair.

"Oh, that's too bad," said Tate, feigning sorrow for their predicament. But both men knew he wasn't accepting their story and definitely wasn't feeling sorry for them. They grumbled at his remark and reached for the fire again, Frankie pulling his buckskin shirt off his shoulder to look at his wound.

"I need to fix this 'fore I bleed ta' death!" grumbled Frankie as he looked up at Tate.

"You ain't gonna bleed ta' death. Quit'cher whining and be glad I didn't put that bullet 'tween your eyes!" declared Tate.

Suddenly both men pulled back, eyes big, as Gus said, "That's a wolf!" looking behind Tate at Lobo as he trotted up beside his friend. The men looked at the wolf, teeth bared and a low growl coming from deep in his chest, and up at the man that stood before them and back at the wolf. Tate dropped his free hand to Lobo's head and rubbed the wolf behind his ears, causing Lobo to drop his lips over his teeth and look up at Tate.

"You're friends with a wolf?" asked Frankie incredulously.

"No, I'm friends with a very hungry wolf. I haven't fed him for a while and he's been hunting for his supper. When he looked up at me he was asking if he could have you for supper. I'm thinkin' about it."

Both men's eyes grew large as they looked at the dour expression of the man and then looked at the wolf. Gus was the first to speak, "You can't do that! It ain't human! It ain't right!"

"Why not? It's probably not much worse than what you two had planned for me. Right? You were going to take everything, probably shoot me and leave me for the wolves and buzzards. So, what's the difference?"

"But, but, we're still alive! You can't let him eat us alive!" cried Frankie, staring at the big wolf whose fangs were once again bared and dripping with anticipatory saliva.

"Well, we can fix that," said Tate, raising his Colt.

"NO! NO!" screamed Gus, trying to scoot back, pushing with his feet and his hands as he drug his rear end to get away from the fire and the man and his wolf.

"Stop!" declared Tate at the nervous men. "The more you try to get away, the more he'll want to attack!" The men instantly froze in position, looking very awkward with both hands flat on the ground and legs extended before them.

They looked up at the man, not knowing what to expect. "Here's what I'm gonna do," said Tate as he began to explain what was going to happen to the men.

ALTHOUGH HE HAD PLANNED to spend the night in this camp, Tate now sat astraddle Shady and looking down at the men. He had tied them together, back to back, with their legs stretched out and feet tied to opposing trees. He spoke to the men, "I'm leaving one pistol there on the log. After you work your way free, you'll have that, and I'll leave your other gear about a mile or two down this trail. So, I suggest you get your gear and go some other direction. If you follow me, next time I won't go so easy on you. I'll either let Lobo have his way or I'll just shoot you and give you to the buzzards, although I'm not too sure they'd want your sorry hides." He looked at the men, shook his head, and reined the grulla around to take to the trail by starlight.

CHAPTER FIVE
MAGGIE

HER FIRST SIGHT OF BENT'S FORT WAS NOT WHAT SHE HAD expected. She had heard of forts from colonial times and other stories of forts built in the far north towards Canada and others west of the Mississippi. Those images in her mind were of log palisades and uniformed soldiers standing guard. But the adobe walled structure was not only different, it was much larger than any structure she had ever seen before. Even the big buildings and warehouses on the riverfront of Westport Landing, Missouri, where she had worked as a clerk for Pierre Choteau, were dwarfed by this massive fort. With walls standing at least fifteen feet high, and as she would later find out, four feet thick, and bastions on two corners standing even taller, it was an intimidating fortress indeed. The large wooden gates of heavy timbers added to the appearance of a medieval castle citadel. Surrounding the fort were several Indian camps with many of the youngsters playing and running about as naked as the day they were born.

Margarite O'Shaunessy looked to the man seated beside

her on the seat of the freighter wagon and asked, "Mr. Bent, are those wild Indians?"

Charles Bent looked to the high-spirited redheaded woman and replied, "Miss O'Shaunessy, compared to you, all Indians are tame." He grinned and chuckled at the startled look on the very attractive woman. The two had passed the time of the long trip from Westport, Missouri, with friendly banter that both enjoyed. Charles was the older brother of William and together with his brothers George and Robert and their friend Ceran St. Vrain, had started the trading post almost ten years before. Charles and St. Vrain had often made the trips back to St. Louis to sell the pelts and hides gained in trade from the Cheyenne and Arapaho Indians, and to resupply the many trade goods sought by the Indians and others of the wild mountain country. Their fort was the only privately owned fortified installation in the west and was the last stop for the many trade caravans that took the Sante Fe trail to the south.

When Charles had been accosted by the head clerk of the Choteau Fur Company in Westport regarding Maggie, he thought the man was daft. The idea of taking an unattached and unprotected woman into the wilds of the west exceeded even the bounds of his own very active imagination. But when he met the high-spirited and determined red-headed Irish woman, he was even more resolute to have nothing to do with such a hare-brained idea. But he had underestimated the strong will of the Irish and had succumbed to her argument that she had to find her father, Michael Patrick O'Shaunessy, as he was her only living relative.

"BUT THE CHANCES of finding your father, well, nigh unto impossible," pleaded Charles as he looked at the girl over the last campfire.

"Aye, but I've got to try. Me father often said, 'No man ever wore a scarf as warm as his daughter's arm around his neck', and I'm determined to do everything I can to do that again."

"But, you don't understand how big the west is, you can travel for days, weeks even, and never see another white man," he implored, committed to make one last attempt to convince this young woman he had grown fond of, to return to the city.

"It's not another white man I'm looking for, it's me own father. When Mum would sit an' read me his letters with tears in her eyes, she made me promise to find him. It was less than a month after that promise that mum went to be with the Lord in Heaven above and I will keep that promise, with God as my witness!" She slapped her leg to emphasize her resolve, and she looked at the man with her lips pursed and fire in her eyes.

"But the west has killed many a man that was stronger and just as determined as you!" argued Charles, leaning toward the woman, firelight coloring his face.

"There's an old Irish saying, 'In every land, hardness is in the north of it, softness in the south, industry in the east, and fire and inspiration in the west.' And it's to the west I go, for me father wrote of his travels and the places he visited, and I will follow him and I will find him or I will find his grave!"

Charles looked at the woman, took in a deep breath and mumbled, "Arguing with you is like arguing with those six mules that pull the wagon. At least I can whip them to make 'em mind!"

"You even think about raising a hand to me an' you'll be losin' it!" flared the redhead.

"Oh no!" stuttered Charles, "I would never do that, but you're ever bit as stubborn as those mules are!" He tossed the last statement over his shoulder as he made his way to his bedroll. Maggie had privacy with her bedroll atop the many crates in the wagon and with a white canvas cover over the hoops, she felt safe and comfortable. But the words of the man came again and again, as she considered the trek that loomed before her.

THE WAGONS PULLED AROUND to the southeast corner and the gate into the wagon house. Here the six heavily laden freight wagons would be unloaded, and the mules turned into the corral. Charles helped Maggie to the ground and pointed to the door leading to the rest of the fort and said, "Go 'head and explore a bit. I think you'll find it interesting. I'll be along shortly, I'll meet you under the overhang at the central plaza. I won't be long."

She waved at the man as she gathered her small satchel to her and started toward the door. She stepped through the opening into a wide hallway, with stairs leading up the bastion to her left and the walkway leading to the daylight beyond to the right. She started toward what she hoped would be the central plaza, passed a couple of men that stepped aside, tipped their hats and stared. She glanced at them with her hazel green eyes and broad smile and the men stayed rooted in place as they watched her walk toward the plaza.

She seldom noticed the reaction of men as she passed, thinking only of her destination and task before her, but these men were hardened by years away from civilization and their stares were penetrating. She found a chair under the overhang on the east side, out of the way, where she could watch the activity and wait for Charles. The summer months at the fort were the slow months as far as trade activity. With the pelts and hides at their prime in the late fall and winter, most of the Indians and trappers wouldn't come to the fort until late winter or early spring. The many workers, almost a hundred, were glad for the busyness of unloading the wagons and storing the goods and were moving about from the traders' store to the other stock rooms and storage centers.

When she saw Charles approaching she noticed a shorter man with him and he waved from across the plaza. As he neared, he said, "Maggie, this is Kit Carson. Kit, this is Margarite O'Shaunessy from Missouri."

"Mighty pleased to meet you m'am," said Kit, tipping his hat and grinning at the young woman. Maggie stood when they came near and now extended her hand towards Carson. Women did not usually offer their hands to a new acquaintance, but Carson gladly reached out and shook her hand. Charles said, "Ever since we've been travelin' I was hopin' that Kit would be here. This man knows the mountains like no other and if anybody can find your father, he can."

Kit looked to Charles and said, "Whoa up there, Charles. I can't go traipsin' off with no woman into the mountains. My woman is in yonder, 'bout to pop with a baby!"

Charles was surprised at the announcement and began to stutter, "But, but, I was hopin' you could help her. See, her father is the only living relative she has and she's bound and determined to find him," he pleaded, prompting Maggie to give her most earnest wide eyed stare.

"I tell you what. I know just the man for you, I mean, just the man to help you. Tell you what I'll do. I'll send word to him and I'm sure he'll come an' do whatever it takes to find your pappy." He turned and looked at Charles and said, "You remember that young man that made friends with all those different Indians, don't you, Tate Saint. They've been callin' him the Rocky Mountain Saint, cuz he's always helpin' somebody."

"Yeah! I remember him. But, how you gonna get word to

him and how long's it gonna take him to get here?" asked Charles, thinking of what to do with Maggie in the meantime.

"You know, I heard Bridger say he's headin' out that direction an' I'm sure he'll take word to him. So, I'm thinkin' mebbe, oh, month and a half, or two."

Maggie looked at the two men talking as if she wasn't even there and stomped her foot as she said, "Two months! I can't wait two months! I've got to find my father!"

Charles held up his hands and said, "Uh, Maggie, I told you this was mighty big country and two months really ain't long a'tall. Now, you were clerkin' at Choteaus' so, how 'bout if we put you to work clerkin' here and you can have your own room and . . . "

The redhead stomped her foot again, knowing she had little choice, and said, "Show me the room!"

He took a moment as he sat on the bluff overlooking the confluence of the Purgatoire and Arkansas rivers and the fort of the Bent brothers. The fort sat on the north side of the Arkansas surrounded by grassy flats and a few cottonwood trees that sat near the banks of the river. A sizable cluster of tipis to the north told of a band of Cheyenne and another group of tipis and brush huts marked the Arapaho that gathered to the east of the fort and along the river. Tate knew that oftentimes there could be as many as twenty thousand Indians camped near the fort, but this early in the summer most of the bands had gone to their summer encampments and begun their buffalo hunts.

He kneed his horse forward toward the big entryway marked by the massive gates that stood open and inviting. People were bustling in, out and around the fort, packing parcels from the fort and headed to the tipis, and others leading horses into the plaza at the center of the square. As he neared the gate he remembered his first foray into the strange structure and his meeting with Kit Carson, the man that would become his mentor and friend. *Well, I guess I'm*

*about to find out what this 'job' is his message spoke of, I just hope
he's still here and I haven't traveled this far for nothin'!*

He stepped down from Shady, tethered both horses to the
hitchrail and loosened the cinches on both. Lobo had
stretched out under the overhang to await his friend and as
Tate stepped up, he stood and followed him into the trader's
store. Tate paused just inside the doorway and let his eyes
become accustomed to the dim light of the interior and he
heard a scratchy voice from the counter holler, "Hey, get that
dog outta here!"

Tate squinted his eyes to look at the clerk behind the
counter, saw a scuffy looking figure with a rotund belly and
mutton chop whiskers, bald head with a thin friar circle of
hair just above his ears, and a bulbous nose set between
beady black eyes and eyebrows that sported more hair than
both his whiskers and friar circle. He was scowling at Tate as
he stood with hands on his hips and Tate answered the man
as he stepped toward the counter. "Ain't no dog in here, but if
you're talkin' 'bout him," nodding toward Lobo, "he's a wolf
an' I'd like to see you try to get him outta here." Tate leaned
one elbow on the counter and looked at the man and back at
Lobo who stood staring at the noisemaker.

"A wolf!" declared the clerk with eyes now wide and
showing whites as he extended his flat palms and leaned
back as if he could keep Lobo away with his bare hands. "Uh,
uh, . . . don't let him at me, mister. He can stay, sure, he can
stay," he stuttered nervously and backing up another step,
bumped into the shelves behind him.

Tate looked at Lobo, motioned with his hand, and the
wolf dropped his head and moved to the far wall and lay
down beside a couple of sacks of flour. Tate looked back at
the clerk who had slowly lowered his hands and moved back
to the counter, keeping his eyes on Lobo. The clerk looked
up at Tate and said, "There somethin' you need?'"

"Yeah. First off, do you know if Carson is still around?"

"Yeah, he is. His wife 'bout to have a baby, so he's been stayin' real close by. You might find him in his quarters. It's the door just to the left of the stairs yonder," motioning across the plaza toward the corner.

"Alright, then. There's a few things I need, so . . . " and Tate began rattling off the supplies of cornmeal, flour, sugar, lead, powder, caps, beans, and more as the clerk scratched out a list on a flat board before him. "I'll go find Carson an' I'll be back for the supplies," Tate said as he turned to leave. The clerk gave a curt, "Yup," as he began assembling the goods. Tate knew the man would have the order bagged and ready by the time he returned so he quickly exited to find his friend.

"Well, 'bout time you got'chere!" came a familiar voice as soon as he stepped out of the trader's room. Tate turned to see a grinning Carson with arms spread wide waiting to greet his friend. The men hugged, slapped each other on the back, and stood back at arm's length to look at one another. "Boy, it's good to see you! Sorry 'bout White Fawn, I heard 'bout her passin' from some o' the Arapaho hearabouts. Darn shame."

"Thanks Kit, but what's this I hear about Waanibe 'bout to have a baby?" asked Tate, smiling broadly at his mentor.

"Our second!" declared Kit proudly.

"Second? I didn't know you already had one. Boy or girl?"

"Girl, Adeline. Purtiest little thing you ever did see. Fortunately, she took after her mother," explained Carson.

"Now, that's fortunate indeed. If any little girl was runnin' around that looked like you, why, she'd probably scare all the buffalo back to their winter grounds. She hereabouts?" asked Tate.

"Why, sure 'nuff. She's with her momma back at our quarters yonder. You'll meet 'em later, if Waanibe's up to it. But, let me tell you 'bout this job I got for you."

Carson led his friend to a couple of chairs that sat in the shade under the overhang and motioned for him to take a seat, and Kit sat as well. He motioned to a worker that came from one of the storage rooms and cupped his hand to his mouth and spoke. The worker looked up at Tate, then hurried off on the errand apparently given by Carson. Kit looked at Tate and began, "Ya see, Tate, it's like this. Charles Bent, when he went back east for supplies, got hornswaggled into a deal he couldn't get out of, and he brought it back here. He tried to get me to take care of it, but I couldn't, what with Waanibe in her delicate condition, you know. But, I immediately thought of you and knew right away that this would be a job for you."

Tate interrupted, "Now you're goin' round the barn quite a few times tryin' not to tell me somethin' so quit stutterin' and get to the point. Just what is this job?"

Carson looked up to see Maggie approaching and he looked back at Tate and spoke just above a whisper, "Here it comes now!" and motioned toward the redhead as she walked toward the two shade sitters. Both men stood and tipped their hats as Carson looked at Tate and back at Maggie as he said, "Tate Saint, may I introduce Miss Margarite O'Shaunessy of Missouri. Maggie, this is Tate Saint, the man I spoke to you about."

Maggie extended her hand and said, "Finally! I've been waiting, aye, it seems like a bit of forever. So, when can we leave?"

Tate looked at the woman, then to Carson, and asked, "Leave?"

"Well, I was just getting to that, Tate. Let's all sit down and we'll tell you 'bout it." He scampered away to quickly return with another chair. Maggie had already taken his and the men sat, one on either side. "So, Maggie, how 'bout you start by tellin' Tate about your father."

So, Maggie began with the story of how her father had left Missouri just over four years ago to make his fortune in the west. He was determined to try trapping and hunting, and at the same time search for gold. "He wrote once or twice a year, told of his travels and his work. Never made much, but he did send some home. Then me mother died, left me the pittance of their savings, and made me promise to find me father. I said I would. He's the only living relative I have, and I'll be findin' him or his grave or know the reason why."

Tate looked at the girl with fire in her eyes, turned his gaze on Carson, who dropped his head, and back to the girl, "And you two expect me to help you find him, is that it?"

"Aye, Mr. Carson said you're the best one he knows, and he was certain sure you'd be willin' to help a poor girl all alone in the world with no one else." She pleaded with the most sorrowful look she could muster with wide eyes and slightly bowed head as if she were a helpless waif in need of rescue.

"Can you even ride a horse?" asked Tate, already showing his exasperation.

"Aye, from the time I was a wee lass, I've been riding. Whenever me Pap would plow the fields, I would ride the horse. And I been ridin' and huntin' by meself since I was no more'n this high." She held her hand out about as high as the back of the chairs.

"So, you can shoot?"

"Aye, no only can I shoot, I hit what I'm shooting at!" she declared, grinning.

Tate looked at her clothing, and he thought she had gotten both the flared skirt and top from some of the tradespeople from Sante Fe, as it had a definite Mexican look to it.

Although suitable for around the fort, he knew it wouldn't do for the woods and the mountains.

"Do you have any other clothes? I mean, anything different, for riding and such?"

She jumped to her feet, both hands on her hips and glared at the man before her as she said, "Well, of course I do! What do you think I am, a beggar or something? I've got more clothes . . . " and she looked down at her dress and her shoes and calming down, added, " . . . but I guess they're not right for traveling horseback." She put her arms out, hands open and palms up as she looked to Tate with a question on her face.

Tate looked at Carson and said, "I'll get you for this, believe you me, I will!" He turned back to Maggie and said, "Come with me." He looked over his shoulder to make sure she was following, and he walked to the front gate of the fort. As they passed through, now walking side by side, he said, "We'll go to the Arapaho. I speak their language and I'm sure we can get you a couple sets of buckskins," and he motioned to his shirt and britches, "something like this. They usually have some to spare or they can make them pretty quickly. You'll find them more comfortable and more durable."

"Like yours? I can't wear britches!" she declared but didn't stop walking alongside Tate.

"They won't be like mine. Look around, these women are wearing women's clothes, and they're able to ride and not in a sidesaddle. You'll see," he explained.

SHE MADE THE PERFECT IMAGE OF AN INDIAN MAIDEN, EXCEPT for the red hair, fair complexion and freckles. Her buckskin tunic reached her knees and the leggings and tall moccasins completed the wilderness look. They had been fortunate to find a woman of the Arapaho of about the same size as Maggie that willingly outfitted the woman in exchange for a small pile of trade goods including a dutch oven, two blankets, two knives, and an assortment of beads and other trinkets used for decorating their clothing. Now Maggie had two complete sets of buckskins and moccasins from the Arapaho, and Tate had outfitted her with a .54 caliber percussion Hawken, like his, and a hunting knife patterned after the Bowie, but a little smaller. He had also traded an Arapaho warrior for a fine red and white pinto pony and a bow and quiver of arrows. He was intrigued by the construction of the bow, with the main part of the stave made from wood and laminated with hide glue and horn from a bighorn and all wrapped with sinew. She had never used a bow, but he intended to give her plenty of instruction and practice. All of that had cost him twenty dollars' worth of trade goods from the store at the fort, but he thought he had made a good deal, all things considered.

Tate led off with the pack horse trailing behind and Maggie fidgeting as she tried to find a comfortable position on the new saddle and new pony. She had always enjoyed riding when it was just for fun or a short jaunt into the nearby village, but now she knew that a long journey lay before them and there was no way of knowing how far they would travel before this chapter of her life would end.

She looked about her to examine her gear. Beneath the fender of the saddle at her right leg hung the scabbard that held the Hawken. The powder horn and possibles bag were hanging from the stock that extended from the scabbard. On her left side, the quiver of arrows with the unstrung bow standing among the arrows, hung from the strap beside the pommel. Behind the cantle was her bedroll riding atop the stuffed saddle bags. Her additional clothing and grooming items and a few other necessities were in the bags, and her other set of buckskins were rolled up in the bedroll. What Tate had called a parfleche sat atop the saddle bags, behind her bedroll. She didn't remember what was in that, but she was certain it was necessary. She felt herself well prepared and equipped for this adventure, and she was anxious to find her father.

Dear Maria,

I'm sorry it has taken so long to write. It has been a hard trip. I got a job with a group of freighters going to Sante Fe. They made me a teamster and relief driver. It was hard work and a long journey. I write this from a place called Bent's Fort. I will leave on my own to go to the far mountains. The man with the freighters, a brother of the men that started this trading post, Charles Bent, said I would have the best luck at trapping if I followed the Arkansas River to the mountains. He also said I should look for gold in the streams from the mountains. I am hopeful of a good bounty of furs and maybe if the Lord wills, some gold.

I have sent you $40. I know it is not enough, but it is the best I can do for now. Give my love to Margarite and you know you have my love too.

I will write again as soon as I have news. Keep me in your prayers and I will keep you in mine.

All my love,

Michael Patrick

Maggie had always been proud of her father. As a young man, his mother convinced him he should become a priest and made sure he had as much education as was available. But when it came time to go to the seminary and enter the priesthood, Michael Patrick O'Shaunessy ran away and took passage on a ship bound for America in exchange for his labor as a deckhand. It was in America that he met and fell in love with the daughter of a Spanish Don visiting the East on a buying trip for the new breed of black cattle called angus. Maria Alisa Della Rosa was taken with the big red headed Irishman and contrary to her father's wishes, ran away with the man. After many different jobs including stevedore on the docks, a stump-puller on the Erie Canal, and as an assistant constable for the city of Chicago, his failure to fulfill his promises to ply her with riches greater than her father, prompted his journey to the west in search of those riches.

Maggie kicked the pinto up alongside Tate and his grulla, looked over at the man and said, "So, what do you think of my father's letter?" He had started reading the stack of letters once they lined out on the trail.

"Interesting. But doesn't say much. Do the others give more detail as to his whereabouts?" answered Tate.

"Well, I'm not sure. They might mean something to you, I don't know about the names of places and such. But there's not a lot. He usually spoke of his hopes and dreams and wanting to be back home. You said we were going to the place where me father first went into the mountains, is it far?"

Tate reined up, leaned forward with his forearms crossed on the pommel of the saddle and looked at the redhead. She was a very pretty woman, he guessed her age at about seventeen or eighteen, with long red hair that hung past her shoulders. Her fair complexion was dotted with freckles that added what Tate thought was a kind of glow, accented by dimples in both cheeks. Her green eyes, what one poet had called the windows of the soul, flashed with mischievousness, fire, and a blend of joy and peace, surprising for a woman in search of her father. Tate had yet to see any fear in the woman, but ample determination, stubbornness and spirit. Her new buckskins did little to hide her feminine features, which were plenty, and he let a grin of appreciation cross his face.

"Look lady," he began but was quickly interrupted by the redhead as she said, "Aye, I am a lady, but me name is Margarite, Maggie if you prefer. And I'll be thanking you for being called by me name instead of what I am."

"O.K., Maggie. You will note, we have no clocks, hourglasses, or even calendars. Time is measured in years, seasons, or even phases of the moon. But, we have no way of keeping track of what month or day it is, except our own memories. Now, as to when we'll get somewhere, there's just no telling. Because, we don't even know where we're going, so we don't know when we'll get there. I can tell you this. If we're careful, and fortunate, and the Good Lord is willing, we will make it to someplace to camp for the night, and hopefully have something to eat before we try to get some sleep. And if we're careful, and fortunate, and the Good Lord is willing, we'll wake up in the morning and start again.

Everything in this country will either stick you, sting you, bite you, kick you, claw you, pluck your eyes out or try to kill you. And if that doesn't get you the weather will try to drown you, bake you, freeze you, or bury you. So, if we're careful, and fortunate, and the Good Lord is willing, we'll make it somewhere, but for right now, I just don't know where."

She sat silent for a moment and gazed at the man before her, obviously thinking about what he said and asked, "How long did you practice that little spiel before you let it fly?"

"How long have we known each other?"

"Three days," she answered.

"That's how long," he explained.

"Oh," she said softly and dropped her head.

Tate sat up, let the reins hang loose in his hand as he pressed his knees to Shady's sides to start off, motioned with his hand to send Lobo ahead, and waved for Maggie to ride beside him. He smiled at the girl and said, "You'll do." She flashed a smile in return, lifted her head and looked at the disappearing tail of Lobo, as he ducked behind a big sage, chasing a jackrabbit.

"So, Mr. Saint, ye still hav'na tol' me how we're gonna find me father. Ye been showin' me all these ways o' doin' things, but ye've said little 'nuff 'bout me father. Would ye care to be tellin' me?" asked the redhead as she sat comfortably aboard the pinto mare. She had become accustomed to the shuffling gait of the horse and Tate watched as her hips moved with rolling gait of the mare, but Maggie's torso seemed to be totally immobile. That is, except her mouth, he thought the woman had some incessant compulsion to always be talking, but he grinned at the thought. He had become comfortable with her Irish brogue that he noticed was sometimes more pronounced than others. He had also noted there were times when she seemed to speak without any accent whatever.

They had been on the trail almost a week, first following the Arkansas River until it neared the deep canyon and then turning to the south to bypass the long gorge. At most camps, Tate had Maggie use either her Hawken or the bow to practice repeatedly so she would become more comfortable and proficient with both weapons. He was pleased when she quickly learned and revealed a natural skill with both. He had often thought that some had that inane ability that enabled them to become comfortable and skilled with weapons while others could practice endlessly and still lack the coordination to ever become capable. But Maggie had quickly become comfortable with both weapons and he had allowed her to take a young buck with her bow to add to her confidence.

She had also shown a willingness to learn other skills of the wilderness, identifying plants and animals, tracking, recognizing the calls of animals and birds. Maggie had even shown an eagerness about learning how to smoke the meat and care for the hides. In just that week, she had learned much and Tate's respect for the woman had grown as well.

He turned in his saddle, cocked his leg over the saddle horn and looked at the woman. "I haven't told you because I'm not rightly sure. Like I said at the outset of this little jaunt, we'll be takin' it one day at a time. From what I've read in your father's letters, he wasn't too sure about where he was when he wrote them, so I figger the best we can do is to follow in his tracks, as much as is possible, that is. His first letter said Charles Bent had suggested he go up the Arkansas to the mountains and see 'bout trappin' and lookin' for gold. Now, I talked to Charles 'bout your father and he sorta remembered the man, but he didn't remember what he told him. But I've heard Charles talk 'bout how he thinks there'd be gold in the mountains near the headwaters of the Arkansas, and he's often said he thought the place to find it would be up near timberline. Stands to reason, cuz most o' the time any gold is found, it's in a stream and been washed down from higher up. Anyhow, I been thinkin' the best way is to try to follow in his footsteps an' start in the mountains where they be near the upper reaches of the Arkansas."

"Well, why did we leave the river, then?" asked Maggie,

wondering about their recent change of direction. She knew he said something about a canyon, but they were quite a way south of the river now.

"That river, the Arkansas, cuts through the hills yonder, and they be mighty rocky hills, and it would be impossible to follow the river through that canyon. That is unless we were riding bighorn sheep, which we ain't. We'll come back to the river, oh, 'bout a week or so. We'll be travelin' along those mountains you see behind me, yonder." He motioned over his shoulder with his thumb, "Not those little'ns right'chere, but them big'uns with the snow, yonder. Those are the Sangre de Cristo mountains, an' they stretch all the way up to the Arkansas River valley." He swung around and dropped his off-side leg down and stuck his foot in the stirrup, as he looked at the far range of mountains. They looked like a row of sculpted granite peaks, lined up like a picket fence, white-washed with snow and with the bottoms draped with a deep blue serape. He looked back at Maggie, a wide grin splitting his face, and asked, "Ain't they pretty?" motioning with a head nod toward the distant mountains.

"Aye, they be that. But I feel in my spirit they be fearful, maybe e'en dangerous," replied the girl with a touch of fear showing in her otherwise fiery eyes.

Tate wondered at the woman. He hadn't seen any indication of fear in her before and now at the sight of snow-capped mountains, she pulled aside that cloak that had hidden her emotions before and gave him a glimpse within. And he knew he was just beginning to see this woman and his wonder deepened.

This camp was their first in the pines. The early part of their journey had taken them across the plains where the only trees were scattered juniper and piñon, and an abundance of cacti of many kinds. But now they were into the foothills of the Rockies and the vegetation was different in these slightly higher elevations. There was the ever-present juniper, but now there were also ponderosa pine and spruce and fir. The sage had been replaced by chokecherry, willow and scrub oak. The higher they climbed, the cooler it became, and Tate sucked in a deep breath and pronounced the air as 'mountain air' made so by the sweet smell of pine.

The routine of making camp had become well-established. Both would strip packs and saddles from the horses; Tate would take them to water and either stake them out or hobble them, while Maggie began preparing the fire ring and makings for the evening meal. Tate would usually return with an armload of firewood and would start the fire and would help in the preparing of the meal. Maggie was quickly learning about campfire cooking, although she believed she was an excellent cook in her own right, but the differences between campfire and stove were many. Also, some of the things Tate prepared, or showed her how to prepare, were new to the lassie from the east. To put Indian potatoes, turnips, cattail tubers, and other wilderness vegetables, directly into the coals of the fire was unknown to her, but the results were definitely pleasing. But when Tate wrapped the trout in the wide leaves of sage and dandelion and placed it in the coals, she was very surprised, but delighted with the result.

When Tate returned with the firewood, he had a good hand full of Camas bulbs and once the fire was well under way and a good bed of coals was glowing, he pushed the bulbs into the coals and grinned at Maggie as she shoveled coals to the top of the dutch oven that held her freshly prepared biscuits. Four nice venison steaks hung over the flames, impaled on willow sticks and dripping into the fire. Both Maggie and Tate sat back and leaned against the big grey log with their feet stretched toward the heat. Lobo had run off on a hunt for fresh meat of his own and Tate and

Maggie were enjoying the idle moment. They assumed similar postures, arms crossed over their chests, smiles on their faces and a glassy eyed stare looking to the campfire. Maggie said, "I never thought I'd be in the mountains o' the west, anticipatin' a meal o' the wild, and sittin' next to a man I hardly know, an' enjoyin' ever' minute of it!"

Tate let his smile spread as he pondered on her words, "Aye, an' for sure, the mountains get in your blood, don' they lassie?" imitating her Irish brogue.

She grinned at him and said, "If'n ye be tryin' to woo me wit' your brogue, ye' got a long way ta' go, an' ye' seem to a' been polishin' the blarney stone, fer sure."

They both laughed aloud, enjoying the moment of mirth. "Well, I have found the mountains do make everything better. Although more challenging, it just seems you can see farther in the clear air, hear more of the creatures of God's creation, and appreciate the vastness and the beauty of His handiwork."

Maggie's glassy eyed stare didn't change, but she nodded her head in agreement to the philosophical assumptions of the man beside her. "I'm beginning to understand the call of the mountains that seemed to always beckon my father. E'en though he'd ne'er been here b'fore, his heart was always here. I don' believe he'd ever have come home to us, but I do believe he'd have sent for us. He loved us, that he did, an' ne'er did I doubt it."

Maggie was pleasantly surprised at the sweetness of the camas bulbs and asked, "Will you show me where to find these? They are wonderful!"

Tate grinned as he agreed to show her and cautioned her, "There is also a plant that looks much like this, only it is deadly. The good one has a blue blossom and the deadly one a white blossom. But, I'll show you."

With the meal over, camp moved about two miles from

the fire and both in their bedrolls, Tate looked at the stars as he prayed, but was interrupted by a scream from the darkness. Maggie sat upright and asked in a strong whisper, "What was that?"

Lobo, lying beside Tate, jumped up and was facing the direction of the scream. His hackles were raised, and a low rumble came from his chest as he peeled his lips back to show his fangs. Tate put his hand on the neck of his friend and spoke softly to Maggie, "That was a mountain lion, or cougar. Some even call them panthers or panter. That scream was his announcement that this is his territory and we are intruding. He probably got a whiff of Lobo or our horses and might even be on a hunt, probably for horsemeat."

"Well, we can't let him get our horses!" declared the woman, as she kicked back the blankets to reveal her firmly held Hawken.

The woods had gone silent at the scream of the cougar, and Tate rose from his blankets looking to the horses. He had brought them close in and tethered them to a picket line stretched between some trees, but they stomped nervously, and Tate watched as they flicked their ears back and forth, listening for any sounds of danger. Lobo stood beside his master, leaning against his leg to show he was near and alert. Tate moved only his eyes as he searched the moonlit trees and clearing. Nothing moved besides the horses. He motioned for Maggie to stay at her blankets and he and Lobo began a stealthy walk to the tree-line below them.

Their camp was on a high shoulder and was surrounded by thick timber. The location was good for cover and camouflage, but the nearness of the thick timber was also advantageous for any attacker. He had chosen this clearing for the view of the valley below and being open for about twenty yards in any direction. They had their bedrolls near the trees on the uphill side, and Tate now moved to the promontory at the lower edge of the clearing. The cry of the cat had come from below them, or across the narrow cut between the hills.

Soon, the sounds of the night returned. The high-pitched *peent peent* of the nighthawk was answered by the deep throated *whoo whoo* of the great horned owl. Cicadas began their clattery chirp and from the bottom of the cut where there were beaver dams, came the *ribbit* of frogs. Tate relaxed and turned back toward the camp, Lobo took off at a run, and the scream of a horse was followed by the sudden blast of the Hawken that split the night. When Tate came running to the camp, he saw Maggie standing and nervously reloading her rifle, stealing quick looks toward the horses. The light of the moon was filtered through the branches of the tall ponderosa, but still showed the nervous horses. Lobo had disappeared into the darkness, obviously in pursuit of something. Tate breathlessly asked, "What was it?"

"Uh, uh, I'm not sure! It musta been that cougar thing you said, I saw a flash of yellow and a shadow and I shot. I was afraid I'd hit a horse, but when it screamed, I had to shoot!" she explained, looking wide eyed at Tate.

"Reload and stay here!" he ordered as he trotted toward the horses, now more jittery than ever. He walked up to them, speaking softly to reassure them, and stroked their heads and necks, looking for any injuries. In the dim light, he could see no obvious wounds, and assumed the horses had kicked at the attacker before he could reach them. He looked around at the ground, searching for tracks, but the grey glow of moonlight prevented his finding any sign. Until he knelt down and reached toward the ground and a dark spot on the dirt. He touched it. *Wet! Maybe blood!* He lifted his wet finger to his nose, sniffed, and nodding his head, he glanced toward the woman and smiled. *She hit it! Now, where's Lobo? I better follow him a bit in case he gets into trouble.*

CHAPTER NINE
ANGEL

LOBO TROTTED BACK TO TATE SHORTLY AFTER THE COUGAR had disappeared. The smug expression on the wolf's face spoke of triumph, canine over feline. There was no blood or wounds of any kind and Tate assumed Lobo had been successful in chasing the cat away. They walked together back to the camp, greeted by Maggie, still holding the Hawken at the ready.

"Did you find it? Is it dead?" she pleaded.

"No, but I think Lobo sent it on its way. I'm sure we won't be bothered again. You did hit it, there was a bit of blood on the ground over there, but it wasn't hurt bad enough to keep it from hightailin' it outta here. I think we can sleep well without worryin'." He looked down at Lobo, seated beside him, rubbed the scruff of his neck and added, "Lobo'll keep watch for us, won'tcha boy?"

Maggie lowered her rifle to hang at arm's length and let a smile of relief paint her face. She walked toward her bedroll as she said, "I'm all for that, aye, that I am."

DEAR MARIA,

I dinna know when I'll post this letter. I will write as I can and it might be that several letters come at once. But I want you to know what I'm doing.

When Mr. Bent told me to follow the river to the mountains, he told me about a mountain with an angel. I couldn'a hardly believe him, but when I came to this valley, there on the mountains to the west was an angel of snow. Her wings were spread wide and she lay in the valley between two points on the high mountain. Never have I seen such a sight, but it was good to see. Bent said I was to try to trap for beaver and look for gold behind the angel. So, that is what I'll be doing. What a wonder it will be to find wealth with an angel pointing the way! Pray for me as I pray for you and little Margarite.

All my love,

Your Michael Patrick O'Shaunessy

"So, did he ever say how he got all these letters out to you?" asked Tate as he stuffed the letter back into the envelope.

"Like he said, sometimes several letters came at once. He said he would send letters by others or when he went for supplies, he would post them his own self. One time we got four letters that he had written over several months," explained Maggie.

"Well, like I said when we started, there ain't a lot of things in these letters that tell of where he is, and a few give tidbits that tell where he was. I'm hopin' we'll find something else along the way that gives us a better idea, but we sure don't have much to go on. Now this letter," lifting the envelope before him, "at least gives us a starting point."

"Have you seen this mountain with an angel?" asked the redhead.

"No, I haven't. But I've heard others talk about it. If it's where I think it is, we'll probably see it later today. The trail we're on follows the Sangre de Christo to the beginning of the range, and from what I've heard, that's where we'll find the angel on the mountain. It's on a mountain range known as the Sawatch and it overlooks the valley of the Arkansas River," explained Tate.

It was early afternoon when the trail took them from the granite peaks to a big hump of a mountain covered with pines and aspen. From that mountain, that held an abundance of clear grass covered parks, the trail dropped to the valley floor and gave the travelers a sense of being miniscule figures on the massive canvas of God's handiwork. To the west and south, the valley was framed by the sculpted granite peaks of two mountain ranges. To the north and east, a cavalcade of rocky hills dotted with juniper and piñon marched alongside the twisting Arkansas upstream, pointing the way to the northernmost mountains of the Rockies.

The fertile and green valley of the bottomland of the Arkansas held an abundance of game. Deer were the most populous, but occasional small herds of elk, a few antelope, and a small game, all made their home in the valley. An ancient Indian trail, used by many different tribes, mostly Ute, cut diagonally from the southwest to the northeast across the valley floor. This trail had been used in the migration routes to different seasonal encampments by the natural hot springs in this valley and other valleys farther north.

Once the trail broke from the timber, Tate and Maggie found themselves on a broad plateau overlooking the valley below and the mountains that lined out on the west edge of the valley. "Look! There's the angel! Just like he said! Well, I think it's the angel, it looks like one of the wings is melting away, but it still looks like one. See it?" she asked excitedly, standing in her stirrups and pointing to the mountains to their left.

Tate looked in the direction she was motioning, grinned

and answered, "Looks like an angel to me!" There, nestled between two high peaks of the first mountain of a long range of towering peaks, was the white form fashioned by the snow. It appeared as a feminine figure, arms with wings outstretched to each side, long hair reaching to the highest peak, and a wispy gown of white that hung to her feet. It was an unusual sight and both Tate and Maggie sat a moment, just looking at the image.

"I'm told the Ute Indians have a legend about that angel," said Tate in a soft voice as if he was hesitant to break the spell of the moment.

Maggie turned to look at the man and with a wide smile, "Tell me, please?"

"Let's step down and give the horses a rest, an' I'll tell you what I know."

They loosened the cinches and let the horses move freely to find their graze. Both Tate and Maggie found seats on a broad flat rock in the shade of a large juniper and Tate began to tell of the legend.

"As they tell it, long ago there was a severe drought in the valley and the Ute people had made their home here. Because of the drought, many died, and the daughter of the chief was broken-hearted to see so many of their people waste away and cross over. She went to pray at the base of that mountain and asked for water for her people. It is said their God of Plenty answered and said he would give them water, but she would have to give herself as a sacrifice. She agreed, and the God of Plenty placed her on the mountain to hold the snow and ice from each winter and slowly melt away to provide water for her people every summer for all of eternity."

The big eyes of the redhead were filled with tears as she turned to look at the mountain and the angel. She whispered, "That's beautiful, aye, beautiful."

Tate dropped his head and gave the girl a moment to gather herself. He stood and took a couple of steps toward the valley and searched the distant mountains for the route Maggie's father had taken. Just to the left or south of the mountain with the angel, a deep cut marked the path of a stream that came from the range of granite peaks. As he looked, he could tell that had to be the valley that drew Daniel O'Shaunessy in his search for beaver and gold behind the angel.

He looked back at Maggie, now smiling at him, and pointed to the cut in the mountains to the west, "I'm pretty sure that has to be the way your father went to get behind that angel. From what I can tell, I think that's where the smaller fork of the Arkansas comes from, so, we'll head that direction for now."

Maggie stood, dusted off her tunic and said, "I'm ready."

THEIR CHOSEN CAMPSITE sat in a small grove of cottonwood next to the creek bank in the valley bottom. Timber covered hills rose on both sides to frame the grassy valley with the shallow but swift running creek. Tate finished hobbling the horses and walked back to the camp. "We'll have a bit of a rest here, maybe till 'bout noon tomorrow. The horses need a good rest and we can maybe get some fresh meat, maybe even smoke some. Whatchu think?"

"You're asking me what I think? I know I've learned a mite o' things since we been journeyin' through this country, but I'm countin' on you to do the thinkin'!" declared Maggie, grinning at the young man who she had discovered had more than a little bit of mischief in him.

"Well, how 'boutchu goin' huntin' and gettin' us some fresh meat?" suggested Tate, soberly.

Maggie looked at him, surprised, but curious, and

answered, "Alright. I'll go hunting, as long as Lobo goes with me!"

Tate looked from the girl to the wolf and asked, "Lobo, you willin' to go with the lassie?"

The wolf jumped to his feet, opened his mouth in what could only be described as a grin and looked from Tate to Maggie, tail wagging. "Alright then, you two go get us some fresh meat. Lobo, you be sure to take care of that girl, now, unnerstand?" directed Tate with a stern look at his wilderness pet.

Just a few minutes after the fearless duo of hunters disappeared in the brush along the creek bank, Tate was startled when he heard in quick succession, a growl followed by a bark, a scream, and a rifle shot. He jumped to his feet, grabbed up his Hawken and ran to the trail taken by the redhead and Lobo. He had only gotten a few steps, when he was stopped by the yelling and whining of both woman and wolf. The overwhelming reek of skunk reached Tate before the woman did and he stumbled back a couple of steps.

Maggie was staggering towards him, one hand holding the muzzle of the Hawken and the butt of the rifle dragging behind. Her other had was wiping at her eyes and she was fussing, complaining, crying, and caterwauling. Lobo followed behind, shaking his head and reaching back to bite at his coat, trying to find relief from the miserable stench.

Tate bent an elbow to bury his nose in the crook of his arm, squinted his eyes and pointing toward the creek, said "Go! Now!"

Maggie staggered toward the creek and fell off the bank to splash face first in the water. She came up screaming, "It's ice cold!"

"Stay there! I'll get you some soap!"

"I can't take a bath in front of you!" pleaded the girl.

"Don't take off your clothes! Wash them too!" ordered

Tate over his shoulder as he ran for the soap. He grabbed a fresh bar of lye soap and ran back to the creek. Maggie was standing hip deep in a backwater pool, still holding her arm across her face and eyes. Lobo was standing on the bank and Tate pushed the wolf into the water to join Maggie.

"You two wash. Scrub hard, use some sand and mud too, it'll help. I'm going to get some other things to help with the smell!" he declared as he moved away from the stream, mumbling to himself, "Not that anything's gonna help with that stink!"

Tate had gathered an armload of ingredients; yucca root, sage leaves, and milkweed, and prepared to make a soapy poultice for the stinky pair. With a pot full of the ground and mixed recipe, he walked to the creek to be greeted by a soaking wet Lobo who shook the water from his thick coat, and successfully drenched Tate. Tate knew it was a lost cause to try to stay dry, but he hoped he could avoid the skunk smell. He immediately rubbed the plaster of home remedy all over the dog, saturating his coat, and pushed the wolf back into the water.

"Maggie, rub that into his coat real good an' it'll help you too. When you're done with him, you can use the rest of this on yourself and your clothes," shouted Tate, to be heard over the chuckling of the white water bouncing down the rocks into the backwater pool.

"Is that really going to do any good?" shouted back the redhead.

"Sure! It's what the Comanche use for soap, it'll be good for your hair too! Oh, and save some for after you take those buckskins off. You'll need to scrub your skin real good too!"

"Ahh! You dinna think I be strippin' me clothes off in front o' you, do ye?" she protested, showing a shocked expression from under her sodden red mop.

Tate chuckled at the thought and answered, "Oh, don't worry your little red head about it. I'll be over here, startin' a fire to dry you both off, and there's a blanket here by the pot of stuff."

He turned away from the soapy pair and rounded the bushy willows to prepare the fire. Dusk was settling over the mountains and the darkness would bring a coolness to the mountain valley and the warmth would be welcomed by the girl. With the fire going, he walked upstream, found a cutaway of the bank where the creek made a bend back on itself, and bellied down to do a little hand-fishing. Within about a quarter hour, he had four nice trout laying in the grass.

When he approached the fire, he saw Maggie standing before the flames, blanket around her shoulders with the skin of one shoulder showing, her bare feet and lower legs soaking up the heat. She shifted her weight from one foot to the other, extended the off foot to the fire. As she faced the flames, she opened the blanket to feel the heat on her bare skin.

"Whoa!" shouted Tate, startling the woman as she clasped the blanket tight around her and swiveled her head to see him walking into the firelight.

"You scared me!" she barked back at the man.

Tate couldn't tell if her face was red from the heat of the flames or the embarrassment of his shouted warning. He dropped his head and chuckled as he walked closer. "I thought we could use something for supper," he held up the branch with the trout hanging, "since your hunting trip was unsuccessful." He grinned broadly and snickered a little.

"Well, I'm glad you were so amused at my predicament!" she pouted.

"Uh, you're gonna have to share the fire if you want me to cook these," nodding toward the fish. She stepped to the side but remained close to the flames.

Lobo lay stretched out within the firelight, head dropped between his paws, eyes watching every movement of the pair by the fire. After several rolls in the grass, he settled down to rest after his ordeal with the skunk, and now showed his weariness as his eyelids slowly dropped to shut out the light. The smell of skunk was still in the air, but not as stifling as earlier, and everyone's hope was the fresh air of morning would bring relief.

TATE QUIETLY ROLLED from his blankets before first light, careful not to disturb the freckle-faced redhead who was sounding like a bobcat as she snored and flapped her lips. Tate looked at the woman, smiled and chuckled to himself at the memory of the previous days events. He rekindled the fire, put the coffee pot near the small flames, and leaned back on the log to spend a little time with his Lord in prayer. He watched as the band of grey along the eastern horizon began to take on the colors of sunrise. The wispy clouds that hung low, soaked up the brilliant orange on the underneath sides and turned their grey blankets into pillows of crimson. The valley appeared to catch the shafts of gold, orange and red, and hold them as brushes to color the hills on either side. Tate sucked in a deep breath of the clean mountain air, lifting his shoulders, and stared at the wondrous beauty of the morning's beginning.

With a glance at the soundly sleeping woman, he motioned to Lobo to come along, and he walked away from the camp. He soon returned with an armload of color, tiptoed beside Maggie and lay the flowers at her side. As he moved back, her eyes fluttered open and she looked at Tate standing at her feet, smiling. She lifted her head and said, "And what are you up to so early this mornin'?" Tate nodded his head toward his bouquet and Maggie turned to see. She caught her breath and reached out, "Oh! Oh! Oh! They're beautiful!" Picking up the bundle she began fingering and smelling each of the blossoms. He had gathered some blue and purple larkspur and penstemon, some pale blue and light orange columbine, and a handful of tiny pink moss campion.

She looked up at Tate with a questioning expression and he replied, "Well, I just thought you needed to smell somethin' pretty for a change." She buried her nose in the bouquet and looked back at Tate and said, "Thank you."

THE TRAIL FOLLOWED the creek into the cut behind the mountain with the angel. Several times they found themselves holding to a narrow path on the steep hillside with the water crashing far below, unseen through the thick timber. By mid-day the valley widened, and the trail was much easier, winding through the aspen between the steep mountainside and the calm flowing creek. With many beaver ponds to stay the flow, the chuckle of the stream had been silenced. With fluttering mountain bluebirds serenading the travelers, an occasional red-winged blackbird warbling at them, and the many other sounds of the mountains, both Maggie and Tate seemed to relax and enjoy the beauty.

Something back in the pines caught the attention of Tate and he lifted a hand to signal a stop as he reined up Shady. The packhorse bumped into the back of the grulla but stopped to look in the same direction. The man slipped off his horse, pulled the Hawken from the scabbard and with hand signals told Maggie to wait. He motioned to Lobo to scout ahead and he followed close behind, moving quietly into the trees. Within moments he returned, sheathed his rifle and said, "C'mon, there's a cabin up there, but it doesn't look like anybody's been around in a while. I think we oughta check it out and see if we can find anything interesting."

They led the horses as they walked into the trees, following the same path taken by Tate on his exploratory walk. The rustic cabin, aged to a dark brown with the years, still appeared sound. The roof was undamaged, the one window shuttered, and the door appeared tight. Tate tethered the horses to a tree at the edge of the small clearing, loosened his colt in the holster, and again motioned for Maggie to wait by the horses. The door opened easily, but Tate stepped back, putting his arm over his face to hide his nose. He waved his free hand in front of his face as if to dispel whatever was before him, then leaned into the doorway to survey the interior. Stepping in, he was seen opening the shutters of the window, spoke to Maggie through the opening to say, "You don't wanna come in here just yet. It smells about as bad as that skunk!"

A simple bunk with tattered blankets sat along the left side wall. Several traps hung from pegs above the bunk. Shelves with a few cans and tableware covered the wall on the right, and a small plank table with one chair sat near the middle of the dirt floor. A fireplace covered much of the back wall and a dim shaft of light showed from the narrow chimney. Seated at the table was the body of a man, bent over the table as if he had fallen asleep on his folded arms. He wore canvas britches, galluses, a grey homespun shirt, and hobnail boots. A peg near the shelves held a tattered coat and crumpled hat. On the table was an enamel plate and cup. The stench of death hung heavy in the stale air.

Tate walked back outside and over to the waiting Maggie.

"There's a dead man in there. Looks like he was a hard-scrabble miner, maybe trapper, old fella from what I can tell. Been dead for a while now, that's why it stinks so bad."

"Is it my father? Did he have red hair?" pleaded Maggie, desperate for any news of her father.

"Doesn't have much hair left, but I don't think it was red. Looked more grey to me."

"Whaddaya mean, didn't have much hair left?" asked the woman, looking sidelong at Tate.

"Scalped. But I didn't see any fresh sign around, so I'm sure they're long gone. Reckon I oughta bury him. There's a pick an' shovel at the corner of the cabin there, if you get that," he looked around, searching for a spot for the grave, "and maybe over there beside the cabin, we'll bury him."

"I'm not touching no smelly dead man!" declared Maggie with her freckled nose wrinkled and her eyes squinting in disgust.

Tate laughed at the woman's reaction and answered, "You won't, I'll get him, you just get the tools. You can start diggin' if you want. I'm gonna see if I can find anything that'll tell us who he is." He walked back towards the cabin, shaking his head at the woman that had shown such grit before, now revealing her squeamish side.

He wrapped the body in the tattered blankets from the bunk, and drug it out to the burial site. Maggie had done little to begin the grave but lean on the shovel and look around the small clearing. "Did you find anything to say who he was?" she asked.

"All I found was a few coins in his pocket. Funny thing, I've never seen coins like these before," he nodded to the coins in his hand as he held them out for her to see.

She looked down at the two coins in the man's hand and her eyes grew large as she reached for the coins. She picked one up, looked at it closely and then at Tate. The coins had a harp on one side with the word Hibernia, and the other side had an image of a man. "These are Irish! They be farthings from Ireland! Me father always carried a pouch of these, c'en though they were no good no more! I bet me father was here wit' this man!" She was almost shouting in her excitement as she grinned broadly and examined the coins closer still.

"Whaddyamean, they're no good? I thought all coins were worth something?"

"Na these. Ol' king George said they were no good and na worth anything. He said only English coin was good. That's why me father had a bag full, just to remember the ol' country!" she explained.

"Well, maybe this man was Irish too," suggested Tate, not wanting the girl to get her hopes up unnecessarily.

"No, no, no. You'll na convince me o' that, laddie. These be from me father, I'm sure of it!"

TATE FASHIONED a brush lean-to to serve as a shelter and reflector for the heat from the coals of their fire. Choosing not to use the cabin, with its lingering stench of death for their night's shelter, they had traveled further upstream to find a suitable camp. After their supper of fresh venison taken by Tate with his bow, the two sat back to enjoy the warmth of the fire and discuss the day's discovery. "But, where does that lead us now? If those were me father's, and I know they were, what do we look for now?" asked Maggie.

"I don't think this valley goes very far up here. Lookin' at the mountains, that one behind us there is the one with the angel. So, I think we'll look to see if he had any prospect holes in his search for gold, or if he left anything else around that might tell us more about where he was goin'. If we don't find anything tomorrow, we'll head back out and move on north along the Sawatch range. According to his letters, we know he went north. But if he's still thinkin' gold, that would say he's stayin' high like Charles Bent suggested. But, if he's given up on gold, and just goin' after beaver, then he'll be workin' the valleys and the lower country. That's why I'd like to see if he did much prospectin' up here." He picked up a stick to push into the coals to add to the fire and he thought about their quest.

"So, if we find some, what'd you call 'em, prospect holes?" she asked as she looked to Tate. When he nodded his agreement, she continued. "If we find some, that we think he did, then that will tell us he's still after gold?" He nodded again, agreeing with her comment. She added, "But we won't know for sure, will we?"

"Maggie, the only thing we know for sure is that we've got a long way to go before we find your father, that is, if we find your father. I told you before, this ain't gonna be easy."

"Well, just finding those coins today meant a lot to me. It just tells me that me father was here, and just to hold those coins made be feel closer to him than I have in years. So, thank you for that Tate." She flashed a smile at her companion and moved toward her blankets to turn in for the night.

"WELL, I'M THANKIN' YA FER YOUR CAMP," SAID THE MAN AS HE stepped aboard his strawberry roan mare. He leaned forward on the pommel and looked at the big Irishman, "You've got a good bunch o' plews there, but the price on beaver ain't what it used to be. But if you take 'em down to Marcellin at the fort, he'll give you as good a price as you'll get anywhere." Jean Baptiste Charbonneau sat up straight on his saddle and nodded to the man that had shared his camp and said, "Keep yore topknot on and watch yore back for that bunch of thievin' outlaws. Don't know much 'bout 'em, but they're a murderous bunch!"

"It was good to have a wee bit of a visit wit' you. Mayhaps I'll be seein' you again," replied O'Shaunessy. The red-headed Irishman stepped back and lifted his meaty paw to wave goodbye to his new friend. Daniel Patrick O'Shaunessy had been camped on the lee side of Long's Peak to soak up the southern sun and to trap the headwaters of the St. Vrain creek. When he camped, he didn't know the name of the peak or the creek, but when Jean joined him, Daniel mined his new friend for all the knowledge of the nearby mountains. Jean was on a meat hunting trip for Fort St. Vrain and had worked with Marcellin St. Vrain, the brother of the founder of the fort, for close to three years as a hunter, pelt grader, trader, and interpreter. When Daniel discovered Jean was the son of Sacajewea, the Shoshoni guide for the Lewis and Clark expedition, he kept the man up to the late hours, quizzing him about the famed cross-country exploration. But all Jean could tell him was second hand information, considering he was but an infant during that time.

Daniel had learned the St. Vrain creek had been pretty well trapped out, and after conferring with Jean, had decided to make for the fort to trade off his plews and resupply. It was just a short while after Jean left, that Daniel was on the trail following the St. Vrain creek out of the mountains. He had no sooner broken from the timber onto the sloping flat land than he spotted three men on the trail before him. Daniel had developed the habit of watching the paths he traveled for any sign of recent passing. There had been only one set of tracks and those at least a day old and heading uphill. The Irishman had assumed those tracks to be made by Jean. So those before him had apparently come from some side trail to take the route that still followed the creek.

Always on the cautious side, Daniel pointed his dapple-grey gelding to a cluster of juniper away from the trail. He decided to take his time and avoid a confrontation with strangers before reaching the fort. He remembered the warning given by Jean about a band of pelt stealing outlaws and thought a touch of caution would be best.

Sitting at the confluence of the St. Vrain and the South Platte River, was a fort that resembled the first post where Daniel was originally outfitted for his venture into the mountains. With tall adobe walls and two bastions on opposing corners, Fort St. Vrain overlooked the river and the distant flats that stretched eastward beyond sight. Daniel

reined up to take in the sight of the closest thing to civilization he had seen in some time. Although not his first foray to
peddle his pelts, it was his first visit to this fort, and it was
more imposing than he expected. He led his packhorse with
the two bundles of peltries as he entered the plaza of the
trading post. Three horses were tethered in front of the trader's room and Daniel recognized them as the mounts of the
men that preceded him on the trail. When he stepped down,
he pulled a pair of plews from one bundle, and walked into
the trading post.

The smell of whiskey, pelts, unwashed bodies, smoke and
gunpowder assaulted his nose as he ducked his head to peer
into the dark room. With little difference between this trade
counter and others at different posts, Daniel waited until his
eyes grew accustomed to the darkened interior before stepping inside.

"Well, either come in or get outta the door! You're
blockin' what little light there is!" demanded a voice from the
counter. A black beret was cocked on the side of the head of
a man with narrow shoulders, a homespun shirt, canvas
britches and a dirty leather bib. His wide eyes shone from
under bushy black eyebrows and glinted with a mischievous
smile.

Daniel slapped the pelts on the counter and said, "I've
got two bundles just like 'em on me horse out there,"
nodding his head to the door, "an' I'm needin' a powerful
lot o' supplies, I am." The clerk ran his fingers through the
fur of the pelt, turned it over to examine the underside, did
the same for the second one and looked to the big
Irishman.

"These are prime an' I'll give you the best price I can. If
you're wantin' cash money, the best I can do is one dollar per
peltrie. But if you're tradin', I can do you a bit better."

"One dollar! The last load I was paid two dollars, and that

wasn't more'n a year ago!" protested Daniel, his forehead wrinkling as he glared at the smaller man.

"I know, I know. But the market's done dropped out on beaver an' that's the best I can do!"

Daniel stomped and grumbled, remembering Jean's telling of the lower prices, and finally stopped to look at the clerk, "You got me o'er the barrel an' that's the sure of it. I'll bring 'em in to ye."

"How 'bout lettin' me get started on your supplies while you're doin' that, my friend."

Daniel began rattling off the list from his memory and the clerk, Marcellin, wrote as fast as he could. When Daniel said tea, Marcellin stopped writing and looked up, "Tea? You want tea?"

"Aye, and I be wantin' at least five pounds of it," declared Daniel.

Marcellin looked up at the bushy redhead who had most of the flaming bush stuffed into a red and green plaid Tam O'Shanter, shook his head and said, "I'll see if I can find that much. We don't have much call for tea. But you said you wanted ten pounds of coffee?"

"Aye, I've become accustomed to the drink of the mountains, but I still like me tea from time to time."

With Marcellin busy at filling the order, Daniel turned to fetch his bundles and noticed three men that had been silently watching the transaction from their seats on a bench against the wall by the lone window. With the light behind them, Daniel couldn't make out their faces, but assumed they were the ones that he had seen earlier on the trail.

Daniel came back through the door, one bundle in each hand, and sat them at the end of the counter. The clerk had stopped what he was doing to see the big man tote the heavy bundles into the post. Knowing the usual bundle of pelts would weigh about ninety pounds, the clerk was surprised to see the man carrying one in each hand with no difficulty. In addition, he had a rolled-up bearskin under one arm. He placed the bear pelt on the counter and said, "I'm thinkin' that'll be worth a bit more'n the beaver."

All the while the dickering was going on, Daniel had noticed a new Hawken rifle on the shelf behind the counter and he couldn't keep from looking at it. The clerk watched the big man and saw his interest but said nothing as he continued filling the order. As the counter became loaded, Daniel would take an armload out to the pack horse and return for more. As the clerk finalized the order, he looked up at the big man and asked, "Will there be anything else?"

Daniel looked up at the Hawken again, thought about his Kentucky style flintlock, and asked, "Whatdya hafta get for that Hawken?"

The clerk smiled and reached back for the rifle, handed it to Daniel and said, "That's a mighty fine weapon, yessir. Let me tally up what we've got here an we'll see where we stand."

Marcellin looked at his figures, checked them again, and looked up to Daniel and said, "Well, sir, if we add the rifle in, you come up a bit short." He pointed to the figures and showed how much he was light. Daniel turned and went outside, retrieved his flinter, and came back in to lay it before the clerk.

"If you take that in, what does it tally?" asked Daniel.

The clerk scratched a bit more and turned the slate around to show Daniel. The Irishman looked down, scowled, and said, "All I got is these coins," and showed a handful of the Irish farthings to the man.

After a quick examination, Marcellin said, "Sir, these aren't worth anything here, but I tell you what I'll do, I'll keep one of these and take fifty cents off, but that's all."

Daniel picked up the Hawken, held it to his shoulder and sighted along the barrel toward the front door, dropped the rifle back down and leaned over to the clerk as he reached into his pocket and whispered, "Don't say anything for those fellas to hear, but what about this?" He pulled his hand out and dropped a gold nugget the size of his thumbnail in the clerk's hand.

Marcellin felt the weight of the nugget, looked closely at the smooth knobby gold stone, and lifted his wide eyes back to Daniel and whispered, "I'll have to give you at least a twenty-dollar gold piece to make it even."

Daniel nodded, grinned and said, "That will be just fine, me friend, yes indeedy. Oh, an' by the way, could you post these for me?" He handed the clerk two letters to his wife and daughter. Marcellin looked at the letters, nodded his head, and reached for his money box to make change.

Although the men on the bench that were making short work of the jug of whiskey, made little noise to disturb the exchange, they had noticed what had transpired. As Daniel left, proudly carrying his new Hawken, three men finished off the jug of whiskey, procured another one, and walked out the door to see where the big Irishman was going. As they watched him ride through the big entry, leading his heavy-laden packhorse, the three men grinned at one another and started for their horses.

CHAPTER TWELVE
CHALK-CLIFFS

Dear Maria,

The other day I found a treasure! But it was a treasure of beauty, not wealth. They were pretty blue crystals and I thought if I had a string to put them on to hang around your neck, you would look like a mermaid from the sea with drops of seawater upon your chest. But I found no gold, well, at least not very much anyway.

I left the mountain with the angel and continued alongside the mountain range. And what did I find? A sight that spoke of home! Like the White Cliffs of Dover we looked upon as we sailed from home, there were white cliffs along the mountain. I see them as another sign. I will go into that valley and hope to find many peltries and if the good Lord is willing, maybe some gold. I wish you were here with me to see this beautiful country. It is not as green as our homeland, but the mountains are magnificent and draw me to them. I will write when I can and send what I can.

With all my love,
Your Daniel

THE FLOWERS, tiny and blue, made a blanket for the pair.

Even Lobo rolled in the patch of color, causing both Tate and Maggie to laugh at his antics. They were seated on the sloping hillside overlooking the bowl of green below them. The granite peaks surrounded the valley, reaching skyward as if to carve their initials on the blue canopy. The talus slopes that trailed from the tips of the grey peaks, were covered with tan and dusty red limestone and granite slide rock. High up, they were bare of any timber and fell toward the valley floor to once again accept the cover of spruce and fir. The two were just above timberline and a cursory glance would see only barren rock, but as the two man-hunters could tell, the tundra showed plentiful life.

Tate pointed to a rockpile and Maggie looked, then back at Tate, "What? I don't see anything."

"Look to the right of that top boulder, it'll move."

"I see it! What is it? Looks like a ball of fur!" declared the excited Maggie.

"That's a marmot, or what most call a whistle-pig! Like its cousin, the prairie dog, whenever it spots danger, it will sound a whistle to warn its family then duck back into its burrow. Now, watch closely, that big ol eagle's been circlin' and it's probably gonna make a try for that fat little feller."

Overhead, the wide brown wings of a golden eagle caught the uplift from the valley below and circled silently, watching the marmot. Suddenly it tucked its wings and dove toward the valley floor.

"Ohh, no!" exclaimed Maggie, watching the dive-bombing eagle, and then the whistle-pig. But the marmot did not move, apparently unaware of the threat from above. The fat mountain rodent was sitting up on his hind legs, front legs dangling before him as he looked towards the horses and people on the mountainside. The eagle plummeted toward the rock pile and suddenly disappeared behind the promontory, and within seconds was seen, flapping broad wings as it lifted skyward with a pale grey ball of fur clutched in its talons. At the same instant the eagle neared the boulders, the marmot whistled and disappeared. Maggie watched the eagle gain height, turned to Tate with wrinkled brow and looked for an answer.

"Guess ol' mister golden didn't want pork, musta been hungry for rabbit," explained Tate, grinning at Maggie.

"Did the . . . ?"

"Yup, he whistled just 'fore he disappeared. Musta knowed he wasn't on the eagle's menu."

Tate stood and began to search the surrounding hillsides, saw something interesting and said, "Let's walk over yonder, that might be a prospect hole," pointing to a scar on the face of the slope behind them. Leaving the horses to graze on the tender shoots of the tundra, Tate led the way to the signs of digging.

"Yup, sure 'nuff. Somebody's been diggin' here. Looky there," he pointed to the deepest part of the hole. "That's a seam of quartz, good sign." He stepped from the pile of rock at the edge of the dig, slid down into the armpit deep hole and began scratching at the quartz seam. A change of color caught his eye, and he dug at it with his fingers. Unsuccessful, he pulled his bowie from its sheath at his back and used the tip to pry loose the object of his interest. He brushed the loose soil away, held the rock to the light and said, "This is it! This is what your father told about in that letter!"

Tate held the rock up to Maggie and she turned it over and over in her hand, smiling as a tear came to her eye. When she dabbed at the tear, she inadvertently made a smudge of dirt on her face, and she lifted the blue crystal to the sun. "Oh, my, it is pretty. Now I see what me father meant when he said Mum would look like a mermaid. Aye, this has the color of the sea about it." She looked down at Tate and asked, "Are there more?"

When Maggie extended her hand to give Tate help from the hole, he almost pulled her in with him, but he climbed free with both of them laughing at his lack of dexterity. He handed her two more aquamarine crystals, dusted off his hands and stood to look around. He frowned as he looked at something about ten feet from the hole and started toward it.

Maggie asked, "What do ye see?"

Tate motioned to a pile of rocks as he walked toward it. Four slightly flat rocks, each successive one smaller than the one below, were neatly stacked together. Tate stood with hands on his hips and looking down as Maggie approached.

"Well, apparently the one that made the hole made the stack," observed the redhead.

"Ummhumm, sometimes they use stacks like this as a claim marker." He lifted his eyes to search the hillside, pointed, "See, there's the others. There," pointing to each one, "and there and there." He bent down to move the rocks.

"What are you doing?" asked Maggie.

"Whenever somebody makes a claim, they usually leave something that would identify it as theirs." He removed the top two rocks, picked up something, looked at it and handed it to Maggie.

"It's a farthing! An Irish farthing! This was me father's!" She jumped up and down as a broad smile split her face as she giggled at Tate.

It wasn't until about noon on the second day after leaving the mountain of the angel that the duo spotted the chalk cliffs at the base of another tall granite peak. They had been following the Arkansas River, but the trail bent to the north-west when the canyon made it impossible to follow the river.

"Ooooh, that hasta be what me father wrote about! Those

are white cliffs like he said," exclaimed Maggie, standing in her stirrups and pointing.

"Looks like. But, that's too far for us to try to make today, we need to find us a camp and give these horses some time to rest up. We've been pushin' 'em pretty hard. These dry creek beds don't show much promise, but I'm thinkin' that green up there," nodding his head toward a small grotto, "might have a spring. If there's water, we'll camp there for tonight, maybe even longer, dependin' on how the horses are doin'," declared Tate.

MAGGIE STOOD on the shoulder of the knoll, looking in the direction of the chalk cliffs, still visible in the fading light of dusk. Tate walked up beside her, "Penny for your thoughts."

She dropped her eyes, turned to face the man and said, "Oh, just thinkin' 'bout me father. It's like we're followin' his footsteps, but I'm wonderin' if that's all we'll find, just his footprints left behind, maybe a farthing or two, but will we find him?"

"Now, don't go gettin' all wistful on me now. I think we're makin' good progress. We've already found more'n I thought we would. And, like I've said before, the good Lord willin', we just might catch up to this will-o'-the-wisp that he seems to have become."

She stretched out her hand to put it on Tate's arm, smiled at him, "Thank you Tate. And you're right, we've already found a lot. But . . . " and she dropped her eyes again, letting her hand rest on the man's arm.

He placed his hand over hers, squeezed it, and said, "Maybe we better turn in, mornin's gonna come mighty early."

CHAPTER THIRTEEN
VILLAGE

"I AM CALLED TALL BEAR, THIS IS MY SON, SPOTTED WOLF," said the impressive leader of the village on the move. He held a war lance across his thighs and the withers of his nervously prancing bay horse. The big bay wouldn't take his eyes off the massive wolf that stood beside Tate's grulla. The leader had long loose hair hanging past his shoulders, three feathers, each one notched, hanging from a tassel. A bone and bead breastplate adorned his chest, a metal band encircled his bicep, and fringed leggings sided his breechcloth. The son was attired in a similar fashion and loosely held a bow with a nocked arrow at his side. While the leader's expression was stoic, the son's was a glaring stare.

"I am known as Longbow and this is Margarite of the Irish," stated Tate, motioning to the redhead. He also caught the stare from the warrior as he looked at the abundance of red hair adorning the woman. "You are of the Ute people?" asked Tate.

"We are of the Mouache. We travel the old trail of our fathers to the land of many waters." Behind the man moved a long procession of Mouache Ute, horses pulling heavily laden travois, dogs with packs, children running alongside mothers as the women led the horses. It was a village of considerable size, with a horse herd of at least a hundred and fifty.

Tate guessed the village to have at least fifty lodges, meaning there were probably sixty or more warriors. He looked to the leader as he explained, "And we are traveling to find the father of Margarite," shared Tate, motioning to the mountains. "We know he was in the mountains beyond those white cliffs and we go to find him."

The leader of the Ute looked from Tate to Maggie, down at Lobo and said, "I have not known of any one that travels with a wolf," observed the man. He looked up at Tate and asked, "The one you seek, did he have hair like this one?" motioning to Maggie.

"Yes, and he is a big man, some would say the size of a bear," explained Tate, hopefully.

Maggie stared at the big warrior, breathlessly waiting and hoping to hear word of her father. She looked at Tate and back at the leader of the Ute, anxious in hope.

"Before the long winter, such a man was seen in those mountains. He had a lodge above the white water, but he is gone from there."

Tate grinned at the news, looked to Maggie to see a broad smile and turned back to Tall Bear, "What you tell us is good. We will keep on the trail to find him."

"Then go in peace, Longbow," stated Tall Bear, moving his forearm, palm down, from his chest and away in a sweeping motion.

Tate repeated the action answering, "And you too, my friend. May the great Manitou go before you and give your village peace."

TATE AND MAGGIE stepped down from their horses to await the passing of the village. Taking a seat in the shade of a big juniper, the two watched the procession of native people bound for their summer encampment beyond the hills and near the flats. Maggie smiled at the playful antics of the children, playing some kind of hoop game as they ran beside the caravan.

"I do believe we are getting closer to finding me father. It was good to hear that man say he had seen him, even though it was a year or more ago. At least he was still alive," mused Maggie. Her lifted spirits showed as she fidgeted on the rock, anxious to be back on the move in their search. Tate watched as she wiggled back and forth as if her wishes and wiggles were going to expedite their hunt. She saw his expression and asked, "What?"

"Oh, just you and your fidgetibit ways," he said as he stood, watching the last of the procession pass. He looked down at the exasperated redhead, grinned and said, "Well, let's get goin' 'fore those ants in your pants start bitin'!"

Maggie jumped up and looked back at the rock, expecting to see ants before she realized he was only funning her. She dusted off her tunic and reached for the reins of her pinto and mounted. She dug heels to the ribs of the little mare and took off at a run, Lobo chasing. She lay low on the neck of her horse, laughing at the surprised expression she caught on Tate's face as she sped away.

Tate hollered, "Hey, hold on there!" as he tugged at the lead rope of the pack-horse and gigged the grulla to a gallop to try to catch up with the wild woman. It was just a short while when he pulled up beside a laughing and smiling Maggie, shaking her head as she leaned over the pommel of the saddle. She had pulled the pinto to a stop, and now sat atop the little mare whose sides were heaving from the run.

Maggie looked at the scowling Tate and said, "Oh lighten up! We all needed a good stretch of the legs and that was fun!"

"Alright, you had your fun. Now you've got to pay the piper. Come on, get down, we're gonna walk a while to let these horses get their wind back." He slipped from the saddle and started walking away, leading the pack horse. He motioned to Lobo to scout ahead, knowing there was nothing to see on the low rolling flats between them and the chalk cliffs, but maybe the wolf would catch his dinner. He looked back to see Maggie, still with a broad smile and an occasional giggle, following behind.

It was early afternoon when they stood looking at the towering chalk cliffs. Reaching well over four hundred feet up the mountainside, the jagged cliffs and the shadows loomed like mysterious ghosts of spirits long past. Even the wind moved without so much as a whisper and the silence added to the eerie sense of the strange formations. A sudden clatter of stones above the cliffs caught the attention of the observers and they looked to see several white rumps bouncing up the mountain.

Maggie turned to Tate, "What are they? They're not deer but what?"

"Bighorn sheep. Rocks like that are their playground. They can go where no other animal can follow. I tell you, I've seen them climb cracks between cliffs like they were playing on flatlands, darnedest thing I ever saw. But what's really surprisin' is in the fall, when the big boys get serious 'bout courtin' they charge at each other like batterin' rams!" He balled up his fists and demonstrated the charge by driving one fist against the other, "they knock those big horns together and the sound echoes across the valley, it's like they're havin' a shootin' match. Beautiful!" He grinned at the memory and smiled at Maggie who was staring back at him.

She dropped her eyes and shook her head, "This is an amazing country. Even the animals are spectacular."

"Speaking of animals, we could use some fresh meat. Maybe we can find something a little further on. That's a nice stream coming down 'tween those mountains, might have some trout. Or, maybe we'll see a deer or even an elk or two. How 'bout it? You in for some huntin'?" He grinned, remembering her last attempt at hunting and the run in with the striped mountain kitty.

She laughed at him, knowing what he was thinking, and answered, "I'll cook, you hunt."

When he returned to camp, he had the carcass of a young buck over his shoulders and a grin on his face. He said, "We'll have to stay here a day or two. We need to smoke some meat, we're 'bout out." He dropped the carcass near the fire, sat his rifle against the log, and began cutting some steaks from the back strap. Maggie watched as he skewered the steaks to hang them over the fire and she reached down for the coffee pot to pour Tate a cup of fresh java.

"Did that Indian say me father had a cabin somewhere in this valley?" she asked.

"Well, he said lodge. To an Indian that could mean a hide tipi, a brush hut dwelling, a brush lean-to, or even a camp under an overhang. So, when we move up the valley, we'll just have to keep a watch for anything or any place that might have served as a shelter."

"But if he had a cabin, that could mean he's coming back, couldn't it?"

"There's no way of knowing. It's not like back in the states, most folks there put great store in their homes, and don't stray too far away from 'em. But outchere, a cabin's just a place to keep warm and that could be for a night or a winter. After that, if there's nothin' to keep 'em around, folks just move on to see what's on the other side."

"Other side?" asked the confused girl.

"Yeah, the other side of the mountain. Haven't you ever gone someplace, just to see what was on the other side?"

"Oh, oh, I s'pose so. I guess me father was lookin' for something, wasn't he?"

"Yes'm, that he was," answered Tate, noting the return of Maggie's wistful expression. "Let me ask you something Maggie," said Tate, quietly, not wanting to upset the girl.

"Sure, what is it?" she replied, looking to the firelit face of her friend.

"How's things between you and the Lord? You know, we're travelin' in some pretty dangerous country, had a few close calls already, and might have more. So, if something were to happen, are you sure you'd go to Heaven if you died?" he asked, looking at her expression of interest.

"Well, of course I'd go to Heaven. I'm a good person, an' me'n me family went to mass every Sunday, when we was back t'home," she declared indignantly.

Tate let a slow smile spread across his face and continued, "Oh, I don't doubt you're a good person, I've seen that for myself. And I'm sure you went to mass, just like you said. But, Maggie, it's not what church we go to, or even how good you may believe yourself to be. You see, it says in Ephesians 2:8-9 'For by grace are ye saved through faith; and that not of yourselves, it is a gift of God, not of works, lest any man should boast.' See, it's not based on the works we do, like going to church, being a good person, and so on, but it's through faith, or believing. See," he paused, scooted a little closer to the girl, and continued, "He says that salvation, or being saved to go to Heaven, is a gift of God, not of works. So, if it's a gift, we have to accept it. And if we do, then we can't boast about being good, or going to church, or anything else. All we can do is say, 'I accepted the gift from God.'"

"A gift? You mean He just gives us a gift?" she queried.

"Well, yes. But that gift is eternal life, and that had to be bought with the blood of Jesus on the cross. He died for our sins, so we wouldn't have to, and he bought us the gift of eternal life that He offers us freely."

"Oh, I see. It's so simple. I often wondered just how good I would have to be or how many times I'd have to go to mass. But it's not that, it's just accepting what Jesus did for us, isn't that right?" She looked to Tate for an answer, saw him smiling and nodding and smiled in return.

"So, now I have a question for you. How do we accept this gift of eternal life?"

He answered, "That's the easy part. Just pray and ask. Something like, *Dear God, I know I'm a sinner and Jesus paid for my sins. I ask you for that gift of eternal life now. Come into my life and save me. In Jesus name, Amen.*"

Maggie smiled at her friend and said, "I just prayed that prayer with you and asked for that gift. Oh, thank you Tate, that makes me feel so much better. Thank you."

"See, God had to make things simple so everyone would understand. So, how 'bout us havin' some supper, whatsay?"

Maggie grabbed up the tin plates, held them out for the steaks and watched as Tate dropped the juicy slices onto the blue enamel tins. She scooped up some cornpone on each plate, added a spoonful of beans, and handed Tate his as he poured the coffee. The dinner served as a time of reflection and contemplation and as the coals dimmed and the two sat side by side against the big grey log, Maggie looked to him and said, "Thank you Tate, for everything."

CHAPTER FOURTEEN
WHITEWATER

THE WATER CASCADED DOWN THE ROCKS THAT MARKED THE steep descent beside the trail. Splashing and thrashing, the whitewater appeared as continuous strings of milky liquid that protested every twist, turn, and fall as what had been crystal clear water blended its substance with pure mountain air to show white as it tumbled through the rocky palisade. Tate and Maggie sat still, mesmerized by the beauty of the falling water and the mountains rising on either side. Tate nudged his horse forward to take the zig-zag trail up the steep slope and was followed close behind by the pack horse and Maggie aboard the pinto mare. The splashing water deafened everything around them necessitating Tate's use of hand signals to point out obstacles and twists of the trail. They soon crested the fall of rocks and reined up away from the chuckling stream.

It was late morning and Maggie called for a rest. Tate had rolled them out early this morning and she felt, rather than saw, the sun rise behind them as they followed their long shadows west into the valley between the towering crags. The thin cluster of aspen beckoned with the ground holding a soft covering of leaves. When she sat down to lean against the white trunked aspen, she chose instead to lay back flat on the deciduous cushion.

"Oh, this feels so good! That saddle was getting so hard, I thought I was getting blisters!"

Tate chuckled as he watched the redhead recline on the bed of leaves accumulated over the past several years of fall seasons. He loosened the cinches on the three horses, walked to the shade of the trees and sat down to lean back against the thin barked aspen. He watched a chipmunk scamper to a moss-covered rock and perch himself on top to observe these intruders to his domain. The quick jerky movements of the little rodent made Tate smile. He picked a slightly pink wild strawberry from beside him and tossed it to the noisy little pest, only to have him hike his tail and run. Lobo watched curiously but apparently didn't think the tidbit worth his effort.

Suddenly a clatter of cascading slide rock shattered the stillness and began echoing across the narrow valley. Coming from hundreds of yards above the aspen, the rock-slide continued, reverberating through the trees, filling the wide gap between the hillsides, and a muffled shout or scream rose above the din. Tate and Maggie jumped to their feet, looking through the trees for sign of the rockfall. Dust rose above the treetops and granite boulders and limestone rock came down the chute beside the aspen grove, searching for anything or place to stop the fall. Maggie ran to Tate's side as he snatched the Hawken from the scabbard, unsure of what had caused the turmoil. Tate was thinking man or animal, either could be dangerous.

The noise subsided, only to be accented by random loose stones bouncing down behind the bigger slide. Dust filtered through the trees and Tate motioned for Maggie to get her Hawken and be ready. As the woman stepped behind him, rifle in hand, she whispered, "That sounded like a person shouting or screaming."

"I know, but we have to be careful, whoever it is might have been trying to sneak up on us and caused the slide. They could still be dangerous." He looked back at Maggie, around the small clearing and motioned for her to take cover near the horses. When he saw her in place, he slowly started through the trees, Lobo beside him, searching the edge of the chute that channeled the rockslide. Dust was thick and lingering, but Tate thought he heard a cough. There. Another one. He moved to the edge of the trees to search the rockslide. The hillside was steep and as he stood looking, the whimper of Lobo made him look uphill to see movement. A hand was waving at the dust, making Tate step behind a tree for cover and forcing him to crane around to see. As the dust thinned, he saw the hand again, then a dusty face.

Tate followed Lobo as the big wolf leaped over the rocks and up the steep incline toward the quarry, but the wolf didn't growl or make any other noise, just stopped and looked.

"Ahh, aaaiieee, aaaaawww!" The stuttering sounds of fear came from the entrapped figure.

Tate was quickly at the side of Lobo, "Easy boy, easy." By force of habit, he had the Hawken pointed directly at the figure, then lifted the muzzle and set the rifle aside. He dropped to one knee, looking closer at the dusty form, "Why, you're just a girl! Are you hurt? Here, let me help you outta there? Is there anybody else?" Although Tate wasn't sure she understood, the girl shook her head, eyes wide with fear. Only one arm was free, the other arm and her legs were under some stone, trapping her and undoubtedly causing considerable pain. Tate turned, cupped his hands to his mouth, "Hey Maggie! Come on up! You don't need your rifle but bring a blanket!" His shouted instructions echoed back from across the other side and he grinned as he turned to the girl. "My woman'll be here to help." Tate had moved several of the stones by the time Maggie arrived, but there were others that had to be removed before she would be free.

Maggie was startled by the appearance of the girl, guessing the pretty Indian to be about twelve or thirteen years old. She smiled at the girl to give reassurance and said, "You hold still, we'll get you outta there right quick!" She brushed her hand lightly over the girl's face to remove some of the thick dust and pushed her hair away from her eyes. "My name is Maggie. What is yours?" The girl frowned but didn't speak. Maggie quickly understood the girl didn't know any English, so she tried again. She pointed at herself, said "Maggie. Maggie." Then pointed at the girl, raised her eyebrows with eyes open wide in a question and waited for an answer. With no response, Maggie tried again. She pointed to Tate, busy at moving rocks, and said "Tate, Tate." Then she pointed at herself again, "Maggie, Maggie." She pointed at the girl and gave the same questioning expression but heard no response.

"Oh well, we'll try again later," said Maggie as she began checking the girl for injuries. There were several scratches, bruises, and some cuts, but nothing too bad. She checked for broken bones, but all were sound. Tate finally removed the last large stone, sliding it aside, and awaited Maggie's direction. Maggie looked up at Tate and said, "Can you pick her up? She's pretty beat up and needs some help."

Tate bent down, slipped the girls arm around his neck and moved his under her frail little body and easily lifted her from the rocks. She was obviously very afraid of the man, trying to pull away, whimpering, and looking at him with fear in her eyes. But Tate persisted, being careful to not hurt her and moving slowly. The girl kept looking at Maggie and stretched out her free arm toward the woman, Maggie lightly touched her hand and smiled.

"How 'bout you bringin' my Hawken?" asked Tate, nodding toward the rifle leaning against the rocks.

MAGGIE STRETCHED out a blanket for the girl and readily began cleaning and dressing her many wounds. The girl pointed to her mouth and to the stream causing Maggie to instruct Tate to get some fresh water for the girl to drink and for her ministrations. When he returned, the girl eagerly drank of the water and splashed some on her face. Maggie turned to Tate and said, "I think we need to make camp here. I'm thinkin' the girl is pretty hungry and maybe you need to go hunting while us girls tend to things."

Tate looked to Maggie, scowling and wondering, but when he realized what she meant, his face relaxed and he said, "Uh, sure. Maybe I'll even get us some fish for supper."

"That'd be nice, aye, I think we'd like some fish."

WHEN TATE RETURNED, he dropped the feathered carcass of a large turkey beside the fire and lay the willow stick with five nice trout beside the bird. He smiled at Maggie and said, "There ya go! I caught 'em, cleaned 'em, and now you can work your magic."

She looked at the bounty, and up at the man and said, "Ye dinna expect me to roast the bird, feathers n' all, do ye?"

The girl limped to the pair, saw the turkey, picked it up and started plucking the feathers. Both Maggie and Tate looked at her, then at each other and grinned. Maggie said, "I think I got her name, it be Singing Bird."

Tate looked at Maggie, surprised, and asked, "Now, how'd you do that?"

"Ah, it's just an understandin' we women come to now n' then." She smiled mischievously at Tate and stood to stand beside him as they watched the girl eagerly plucking the turkey. "She's a beauty, is she not?" asked Maggie, looking at the girl. "Do you have any idea where she came from?"

"No, but maybe with a little sign language, we can figger it out."

"Sign language?" asked Maggie, leaning back away from Tate and looking intently at him, impatient for an answer.

"You'll see," he answered and turned to replace his bow in the sheath by the saddle.

AFTER THEY ATE, Tate set about trying to learn more about the girl by using the sign language common among the plains Indians. After a difficult couple of hours, using sign, motions, expressions, a little pantomiming and drawing pictures in the dirt, they understood Singing Bird was from a small village that had been attacked by some white men and everyone had been killed. Singing Bird had been gathering berries when the attack came, and when she heard the shooting, she hid out until she thought it was over. But upon her return, she saw only the white men, and she ran to get as far away as possible. That had happened three days before and she had been fleeing and hiding since. Tate, Maggie and Singing Bird agreed they would go to the village after first light, and all turned in with heavy hearts, somewhat fearful of the morrow.

CHAPTER FIFTEEN
MACABRE

THE SMELL, THOUGH FILTERED THROUGH THE PINES AND ASPEN, was what assailed them first. It had been a long and uphill ride, following the creek through the bottom of the narrow-sided cut between the mountains, and now as the valley widened, the hills pushed away from the stream to allow room for the Indian encampment. Tucked back into the edge of the tall spruce, what had been a lively encampment of women and children was now nothing but a black scar on the earth. The approaching riders sent the carrion eaters scattering, turkey buzzards took flight chased by crows and magpies. Coyotes and badgers scurried into the brush, and a bobcat slinked into the pines. The stench was overwhelming for nothing stifles breath like the smell of burnt human flesh.

Tate lifted his neckerchief to cover his nose as he turned to look at Maggie and Singing Bird. "You ladies might not wanna come any closer. Looks like I got some buryin' to do an' it ain't gonna be too pleasant, I don't reckon." He scanned the scene before him again, then lifted his eyes to the girl and back at Maggie and said, "Maybe you oughta go upstream a stretch an' make camp. I'll be along directly." He started to turn away when Singing Bird slipped from behind Maggie and started toward the remains of the village. Tate looked up at Maggie and said, "Guess she wants to see for herself. You can wait or go make camp . . . " he said as he started to follow the girl, not wanting her to see anymore than necessary.

The remains of four lodges, three tipis and one brush hut, were mere piles of ashes and debris. Bodies were scattered throughout. Scavengers had been at the remains for several days and what was left was unrecognizable. Tattered bits of buckskins and blankets were scattered. Trade pots and broken pottery littered the area. Tate thought it couldn't have been worse if a flat-land tornado had ripped through. He bent to pick up scraps of blankets and portions of the hide tipis, determined to use what he could to gather the bits of bodies to be buried.

Singing Bird had knelt beside some remains and held what must have been a necklace of sorts in her hands. She began chanting a song of grieving as she rocked back and forth, lifting her hands to the sky and letting tears flow down her cheeks. Maggie came to the girl's side and knelt with her, putting her hand lightly on the girl's knee. Bird lowered her hands, looked at Maggie and held out the necklace, a string of beads, quills, and colorful stones. She motioned to the body before them, and with hand gestures made Maggie understand the body was that of Bird's mother. The two embraced and stood to walk back to the horses together, leaving Tate to the task of the burial.

A short distance from the encampment, Tate found a wash-out ravine to use for a grave site. He used a sizable piece from one of the hide tipis as a drag for moving the bodies. He was surprised to find a torn and chewed fringed buckskin coat on one of the bodies and as he looked, he realized it was what remained of a white man. Tate kept count and as he dragged the last to the ravine, he had tallied as best he could tell, seven women, six men, and four children, not counting the white man. He caved the bank over the bodies, carried as many large stones as he could find to cover the soil, added several green branches and rolled down a couple of sizeable boulders from uphill.

He sat down, wiped his face and hands with his neckerchief and stood to walk to the creek. Without slowing his pace, he strode right into the stream, sat down and splashed the ice-cold water on his face and all over. He was dirty, he stunk, but what bothered him most could not be washed away. He ducked under to wet his hair, came up spluttering and wiped the excess from his face as he pushed back his hair. He breathed deep, stood up and started up the trail after Maggie and Bird. He filled his lungs with the sweet smell of aspen and pine, searched the heavens for beauty, anything to fill his mind and body with good to replace the evil. Lobo had chosen to go with the women and horses, not liking the smell of the death camp. Tate walked alone through the trees, following the narrow trail.

The big wolf almost knocked Tate over as he ran to greet his friend on the narrow path. Tate stood firm as Lobo rested his big paws on his shoulders and licked at his face. Tate rubbed the wolf behind his ears and pushed him back to make him drop on all fours. The two walked at a brisk pace to the camp set up by the womenfolk and were greeted as they approached.

"Lookee here what we've got cookin'," said Maggie, pointing at two rabbits turning on a spit of thin green aspen. "Singing Bird shot 'em with my bow!"

Tate looked to see a smiling girl turning the spit for the roasting rabbits. She had the string of beads hanging from her neck, absentmindedly fingering them with her free hand. Tate made a sign with one hand that brought a nod from the girl and a questioning look from Maggie.

"What'd you say?" she asked.

"I just said good hunting. But we'll need to talk some more after supper. We kinda forgot about our primary objective," he answered, looking at Maggie from under his furrowed eyebrows. "Aren't you forgetting we came up here to look for a cabin?"

Maggie sucked in a deep breath at the thought, "Yeah! We weren't even looking!"

"Well, I was, but we didn't pass anything that looked like a cabin."

IN THE WANING hours of light, the three sat near the dwindling flames of the cookfire, Tate nursing his coffee as they talked with Singing Bird. With the same combination of signs, words, drawings and dramatizations, they learned that four white men had attacked the camp. Tate assumed it was when the men were away hunting, and they were ambushed on their return. Bird said they had many beaver plews and other pelts from their hunts and were going to take them to the trading post. Tate had found no evidence of plews or pelts or any other thing of value or use to white men. He shook his head at the thought of the evil work of thieving men that valued things greater than human life. He knew some white men reviled any Indian and thought of them as no different than any other animal of the forest, and those same men thought nothing of killing and stealing from another white man. Evil is evil no matter the color of one's skin.

Tate remembered his father telling him, "Son, it's not what's on the outside of a man that makes him evil, but what comes from within. It's what's in his heart that makes a man a man or a beast." Tate thought, *these were not men, but cowards and thieves, no different than a sneaking egg-sucking raccoon or other wild beast. Actually worse, because most of the animals kill to eat, not destroy.*

They asked Singing Bird if she knew of any cabin or lodge of a big red-headed white man, but she knew of no such man. She did know of a cabin that was not far from their camp, but no one was there and had not been there while their camp was in this area. When she said she could guide them to the cabin after first light, Maggie's face lit up like a jack-o-lantern and her smile was about as broad too.

It was barely mid-morning when they arrived at the cabin site. Maggie was excited as usual and was the first off the horse to run to the cabin. Tate hollered, "Hey, wait a bit! You don't know what's in there!" He swung from his saddle, Hawken in hand, and trotted up behind her and said, "Now, just wait right here. Grizzlies have been known to sleep in cabins, and all sorts of other varmints too, some of 'em two-legged!"

Tate tried to push the door open but struggled. He stepped back and walked around the corner, looking through the cracks of a shuttered window, stepped back and looked at the roof. From the side he could see the roof had caved in and the timbers were apparently blocking the door. Going back to the front, he set the Hawken against the wall, put his shoulder to the door and pushed it in, breaking the boards but gaining entrance. He stuck his head through the door, saw nothing of concern and stepped back for Maggie.

When she stuck her head into the room, she saw the remains of a table and chair, a bunk, and she could barely see the corner of the back fireplace. There was nothing on the one shelf or on the broad shelf used as a counter. The only light came from the caved in roof and she turned away from the cracked door, but something caught her eye. Stuck in the crack between logs and the door frame was a coin. Only the edge was showing, but it was enough for Maggie to grab at and dig free with her fingernails. The coin had been pushed into the moss used as chinking, but was placed at eye level, at least the eye level of Maggie, making it easy to retrieve. Stepping from the cabin door and into the open sunshine, she turned the coin over in her hand and with a broad smile looked up at Tate. "It's an Irish Farthing, me father was here, for sure and certain, he was!"

"Ahhh, quitcher whinin'! It's his own durn fault he caught that lance! If'n he'da hung back like I tol' 'im, he'd prob'ly still be 'ere!" Beauregard Odus Plenty fancied himself the leader of this band of ragtags. He glared out from under the bushy black eyebrows that appeared as part of the greasy black mop that crowned the head that appeared too small for the ill-shaped form it rested upon. Absent anything that resembled a neck, one would think the figure was put together by a child playing with an assortment of odd-sized balls. A tiny one sat upon a much bigger one, supported by two thin sticks that resembled legs, and the strange figure was topped by a mop of long greasy black hair. Better known as B.O., his pompous and arrogant attitude forced his will on those around him and any discord was quickly met by blood-letting that usually ended in the death of the dissident.

"Yeah, I know. Frankie always was a stubborn cuss. He never did pay no attention to what nobody tol' him. Well, at least I got me a horse and a share o' the bounty," proclaimed Gus McGovern. "So, when do ya think we'll catch up with that big redhead?"

"Ain't no hurry, he's packin' heavy and won't make good time. We can let 'im get well away from the fort so won't nobody be the wiser. Since he got all them supplies, we can just relieve him of 'em, an' go on 'bout our own way. He got 'nuff supplies to last us a month or two. By then, we can be a long ways away," explained B.O.

"Wal, at least we got rid o' them plews at Fort Vasquez. I ain't sure that trader believed we got them plews by tradin' wit' them injuns, but he weren't gonna pass up that many plews, for shore," complained Dingus.

Gus scratched at an armpit, "Still gonna miss Frankie. Me'n him been together nigh unto four years. Been all o'er these mountains, trappin' n' such, 'bout the onliest one I got 'long with." He scratched at his neck, picked a hardback from his dirty hair and cracked it between his fingernails.

B.O. looked at the man, shook his head with disgust and thought to himself the nickname of Nits they hung on Gus certainly suited the bug infested man. Nits' scraggly and dirty blonde hair was topped with a badger skin cap, legs and tail still attached, that looked like the varmint had fallen asleep atop the blonde mop. His patchwork whiskers partially hid his pockmarked face, scarred with a bout of smallpox. But his appearance was the best of his attributes, any other traits were outweighed by the stench of his unwashed body.

"Wal, all I care about is gettin' us a jug or two of whiskey! That big Irishman packed out four jugs an' I aim to have one of 'em. I've got me quite a thirst an that li'l bit we got at St. Vrain didn't do much. I'm thinkin' I could down a jug my own self in one sittin'," sounded off the third member of the motley crew. Dingus Dalton was probably the oldest one of the bunch, with a toothless grin, pointed chin and hook nose that seemed to meet whenever the man tried to chew or laugh. His whiskers never seemed to grow and did little to hide the ugliness of his lopsided features. His face appeared as a misshapen wad of clay, pushed and prodded to where it resembled a rotted apple, wrinkled and twisted and was topped with scraggly salt and pepper hair that seemed to go in every direction but down. When he was asked where he got his name, Dingus usually answered, "From my Ma, you idjit!" and no other explanation was offered.

Gus, or Nits as he was now known, had been set afoot with his partner, Frankie, and when they tried to force their will on a younger man, had been disarmed, Frankie wounded, and both were left bound hand and foot until the young man made his escape. Both Nits and Frankie later realized they had been lucky to escape with their lives, but both harbored a dark desire for revenge against the man that had humiliated and disarmed them. Maybe now with his new partners, Nits thought they might luck out and find the young man that had treated them so badly and add to their plunder by getting revenge and relieving him of his goods.

"Hey, what's this?" muttered B.O., as he turned in his saddle and motioned for Dingus to come forward. B.O. pointed to the trail and said, "His tracks are gone. We was just follerin' 'em, and now there ain't none!"

Dingus, the best tracker of the three, dismounted and dropped to one knee to examine the trail. "Looks like tried to brush out his tracks. See thar', where the pine needles is all pushed aside. Prob'ly took a green branch, used it like a broom. I'll walk on 'head n' see if'n I can fin' 'em."

B.O. and Nits stepped down to stretch their legs and give the horses a rest as they waited for Dingus. Within moments, they heard him holler at the two, "Hey, ain't no tracks! Don't know where he went!" He walked back to the others, shaking his head and said, "I saw where he was brushin' things away, but then it just stopped. He prob'ly left the trail in the trees some'eres. Them pine needles cover a trail purty good. I'll hafta kinda circle 'round a spell, but I'll find 'em. Ain't no bloomin' Irish gonna fool me!"

B.O. looked to the fading light and said, "Go 'head 'n look aroun', we'll set up camp o'er yonder," nodding with his head to the edge of a small clearing. "Looks like there's water there. If'n you see some game, take it. We can use some fresh meat. I'm gettin' tired o' this tough ol' buffler we smoked."

Dingus mounted up, nodded his head in response to B.O.'s instructions and reined his mount into the trees to start his search. When the fading light hampered that search, Dingus returned to his partners, giving his report of failure. "But, I'll fin' his tracks soon's daylight comes. He ain't gettin' away, nosir, he ain't."

Nits was the underdog of the crew of misfits. The last to join, and the dirtiest, neither of the other two wanted Nits anywhere near their food so he got the hardest and dirtiest jobs about camp. B.O. had started their supper, frying some of the smoked buffalo and cooking a pot full of beans, but gladly surrendered the cooking duties to Dingus. Nits had taken the horses to water and picketed them in the trees. He was mumbling his gripes as he walked back to the fire.

As B.O. looked over his crew, he thought about them as a group. As is true with any bunch of misfits, because of their general lack of respect for anyone, he knew it was difficult for them to get along with even their own kind. It was not a pleasant camp, every man complaining about anything and everyone, and each thinking he knew more than the next. When they had attacked the small Indian village to take their plews, what had started to be a raid for plunder had become a slaughter of defenseless women and children and an ambush on unsuspecting men. Not that he cared, but when the initial attack had become a bloodbath because none of the men had even the slightest bit of compassion or respect for their fellow man, he had a momentary pause, but quickly dismissed any guilt. He believed the Indians to be nothing more than heathen animals, so he and his godless attackers never considered tempering their barrage of death and destruction. He believed his buckskin clad mountain men were really no different than most others of their ilk that inhabited this vast wilderness. Now they were on the trail of one that could be considered a part of the brotherhood of the Rockies, but to B.O, he was nothing more than the current possessor of what he considered was theirs for the taking, supplies that would see them through another couple of months in the mountains.

IT WAS a feeling more than knowledge. He knew that man had an ingrained sense that when someone is staring at you, you might not understand it, but you can sense it. That raising of the hackles at the back of your neck that makes you think someone is following or watching. Daniel O'Shaunessy had learned to pay attention to his extra senses. He knew it took more than sight and hearing to detect the presence of danger. More often than not it came as a thought, a sensation, a feeling, that something wasn't right. He had watched his backtrail ever since he spotted those three outlaw types in the trading post back at Fort St. Vrain. He didn't know if they followed him from the fort or not, he hadn't seen any sign of them on his backtrail, but when his hackles raised, he chose to act.

On a winding stretch of trail through the thick pines where the path was covered with a thick layer of needles, he formulated a plan. Dropping from his mount, he broke off a long bough from a nearby spruce and used it to sweep the trail for several yards before him. It was obvious with the cleared path that he had swept the trail, but the lack of tracks beyond the cleared area would, at least temporarily, confuse any tracker. He returned to his horses, backed them up, one at a time, several yards back down the pine laden trail. Once both horses were in place, he led them through a thick cluster of ponderosa with a deep carpet of long needles, careful to erase any sign of their passing by repeatedly going back on foot to restore any thing that might give them away. He did this for a distance of almost a hundred yards until they came to a wide stretch of broad flat limestone where he led the animals across, leaving no evidence. He then mounted up and continued on his way, finding his own trail through the pines and aspen, making his way higher up the mountain to his destination near timberline.

"I DON'T KNOW where he went, B.O., honest! I can't find hide nor hair o' the man. I circled all round the trail, covered both uphill an' downhill for a half mile on both sides an' thar ain't nary a track or nuthin!" whined Dingus, reaching to refill his tin coffee cup with hot brew.

"Wal, he cain't just fly away! He's gotta be some'eres! How 'bout caves or other hidey-holes. Anythin' like that?" quizzed B.O.

"Nuthin'! I'm tellin' ya' the man just disappeared! Ain't never seen the like," grumbled the toothless man, noisily sipping at his hot coffee.

"Wait, I know. If he chose to disappear here, that must mean his cabin or whate'er is some'eres 'round here or at least not too far away. We'll just keep a goin' an' we'll prob'ly come on him down the trail. We can watch fer smoke 'n such. If he thinks he's lost us, then he won't be so careful, 'n then we can find him. Way he's headin' I'm thinkin' he's bound fer Bayou Salado or some'eres round there. Maybe not out in the flats, prob'ly in the mountains round there, at least that's the way he's goin'," declared B.O.

"Why, B.O., that's plumb smart. I'da never thot o' that! But I think you're prob'ly right. You know, I often wondered 'bout that country. I knowed there's several fellers got 'em some nice beaver from them ponds out in those flats, but mebbe thar is some gold back in them mountains," answered Dingus.

Nits was listening to the two men, nodded his head as he thought about the Bayou Salado. Many men had talked about the country and how there was everything a man could want. Buffalo spent summers grazing the broad flatlands, the streams were full of trout and beaver, and the mountains held an abundance of deer and elk. It was beautiful country, but even with all its promise, it still required a lot more work than any of the men were willing to put forth. Especially when they thought it the smart thing to let others do the work and all they had to do was relieve them of the plunder. It was much easier that way. Besides, if the big Irishman had gone farther south, that just put them closer to their destination of Sante Fe, where once they had the right amount of money or goods, they could enjoy life and not have to spend another freezing winter in these mountains. Just the thought of the warm sun of Sante Fe warmed up the scraggly looking old man. Sunshine, yeah!

CHAPTER SEVENTEEN
CHEYENNE

Tate's grin was almost as bright as the coloring on the leopard appaloosa mare he led into their camp. The horse was prancing nervously at the end of the lead rope that Tate had fashioned into a halter and lead, but when Singing Bird saw the animal she jumped and ran to hug the horse's neck and talk to her. She stroked the mare's neck, rubbed behind her ears and leaned back to look into her eyes as she spoke softly to the spotted mare. She turned to Tate, tears in her eyes, and with signs and a few words, explained the horse was her father's. She was considered a medicine horse and her father was the shaman of the village. Cloud Walker, her father, had traded for the mare from the Nez Perce when she was but a weanling and Singing Bird had loved the animal from the first time she saw her.

Maggie had walked up beside Tate and leaned against him, "That's quite a horse. Where'd you find it?"

"Well, when I was buryin' all them folks, I saw a lot o' sign of horses and figgered there had to be some still around, cuz the raiders couldn't take 'em all. When I found the tracks of the raiders leavin', I saw they hadn't taken but a couple horses. So, I just followed the sign, found this'n by the stream yonder and e'en though she was a little skittish, I got a rope on her, and she settled right down an' here we are," he explained.

"She acts like she knows that horse," said Maggie, nodding towards Singing Bird.

"She should, she said she's known that horse since it was little. Belonged to her daddy, who was the Shaman, or medicine man, of their village. That, my dear, is what the people called a Medicine Horse."

"A Medicine Horse?" queried Maggie, her brow wrinkling with question.

"Yup. Don't mean much, really. Prob'ly just cuz it was the medicine man's and it had such unusual markings. They don't see many appaloosas round here, especially a leopard one like that."

"I'm guessing you call it a leopard because of all the spots?" asked Maggie.

"Ummmhummm," answered Tate, grinning. "But at least she's got a horse of her own and you don't have to ride double anymore. It'll make it easier on both of you, and your horse as well."

It was late morning before they were on the trail again. Covering familiar country and going downhill most of the way, they made good time and set up camp by the moonlight in the treeline that bordered a wide park at the foot of the chalk cliffs. By first light the following morning, they had the white shoulder of the towering mountain behind them and they were making their way across the foothills of the Sawatch Range that extended out from the mountains like the legs of a reclining giant. In the Rockies, many of the foothills have one slope, usually the south facing one, covered with thick timber, while the opposing slope shows a bare grassy park devoid of any trees. So, the trail would go from thick trees, to open park and back into the trees as they followed the up and down of the north bound trail, always keeping the granite peaks over their left shoulder.

DEAR MARIA,

I have found some gold. Not a lot, but I did find some nuggets and panned

some dust in a couple of streams above the white cliffs. I hope to get some money to you soon, but as you know, unlike back home in the old country, currency is not used much here in America. I hope to get with a trader that makes trips back to St. Louis for goods, to carry the money to you. I hope to get more, but I will leave the white cliffs behind come spring. I was told of a place called Bayou Salado that should have a lot of beaver and I hope to get many pelts to trade for coin to send to you.

I still hope and pray for a good find with gold and will work all the streams and any other promising place on my way to the Bayou Salado. So, I'm sure I will write again even before you get this letter. As always, I am praying for you and Margarite.

Love always,

Your Daniel

"NOW THAT WE'RE out of the trees and into the flats, we'll be able to make the river bottom by time to camp. Maybe you can go hunting and get us some fresh meat," suggested Tate, grinning.

"You're never gonna let me live that down, are ye?" countered Maggie. Both were remembering the episode with the skunk.

When Singing Bird asked, Tate had to explain using signs and exaggerated gestures to indicate the smell of the skunk. Bird laughed at Maggie's embarrassment, but signed to Tate that the same thing had happened to her. Maggie nodded her head, smiling, at the shared experience and reined up for Bird to pull alongside. The two had been continually working at sharing their languages and now they again conferred, effectively excluding Tate from the girl's only confab.

The flat they crossed was a broad plateau or park that ended with a drop off to the river bottom. Covering about two to three miles from the timberline to the river-bottom, the plateau was dotted with juniper, piñon, sage and cactus with considerable bunch grass and gramma. A few dry gulches or ravines scarred the flat, cut by run-off flash floods that fought their way to the river. A broad ravine had beckoned to Tate with the promise of spring water in the bottom and he pointed the grulla over the edge to slide to the bottom. An oasis of cottonwood and grass promised a comfortable camp with the added protection of the ravine ramparts to hide their presence.

"I think this'll make a nice camp," he looked to the sky and the dropping sun that hung just above the mountains behind them, "and there's plenty of time to do a little hunting. So, if you ladies make camp, I'll see if I can get us some fresh meat."

"Oh, you don't want the ladies to put you to shame and do the hunting and the cooking for you?" teased Maggie.

Tate puffed out his chest, dropped his chin, and put on his most serious expression as he beat his chest and growled, "No, brave man go hunt. Kill game, bring meat to his women."

Both ladies bent over laughing, and Tate relaxed and laughed with them. It was good to have a little fun, to bring relief to an otherwise arduous task of finding Maggie's father and Singing Bird's people. Tate slipped his longbow from its sheath, hung the quiver of arrows from his belt and admonished the girls, "Now, just cuz the big hunter is leaving, doesn't mean you get to loaf, now, get busy." They laughed at him again and he started off down the ravine toward the river.

Although the small spring-fed creek in the ravine had water sufficient for their camp and the horses, Tate knew the river bottom with its plentiful grass, brush and of course water, would have greater promise for deer or even elk. He worked his way down the ravine, staying behind cover wherever possible until he neared the mouth of the ravine. He sat back on the gravely slope, hiding behind a cluster of hill-hugging sage, as he scanned the brush along the river bank. Searching any openings that would give deer access to the water, Tate watched for any movement that would give away animals making their way to their evening drink. Finally, motion near the willows caught his eye. A nice buck and two smaller ones were feeling their way to the water, cautiously placing each foot and watching for any danger.

Tate was about seventy yards from the deer and wanted to get a little closer. He saw another cluster of sage that would afford good cover and get him almost twenty yards nearer. He waited until the deer were focused on their move to the water, then quickly and quietly made it to the sage. When the deer had their fill, the big buck turned back to lead the way from the brush. Tate was ready. He stepped into his bow with the arrow at full draw and let fly the silent missile. The arrow buried itself in the side of the second buck, impaling it just behind the front leg and leaving just the fletching protruding like a large butterfly had landed on its lower side. The buck staggered and fell forward, the other two sprang away and disappeared into the cottonwoods downstream.

Tate rose from the sage, but something caught his eye and he dropped back down. Pushing aside a small branch of the strong-scented brush, he looked upstream from his kill and saw movement. He waited and watched as a line of Indian warriors came from crossing the river and began making their camp. They were about a half-mile above Tate's cover and busily preparing their site. He estimated the party numbered about twenty, all warriors. *That's a raiding party, and from what I can tell, I'm thinkin' they're Cheyenne. That's not good, Cheyenne and Ute don't get along too well, and this is Ute country. Not a good place to be.* He watched for just a moment longer, then in a low crouch, made the mouth of the ravine and began trotting back to the camp.

When he came back empty handed, Maggie said, "Where's the meat?" grinning at Tate's dismay. Then she noticed his expression was not one of joviality and asked, "What is it? What's wrong?"

"We've got company. Looks to be a raiding party of Cheyenne."

Singing Bird had recognized the name Cheyenne and she jumped to her feet, alarm spreading across her face as she looked askance at Tate.

"We'll sit tight right here till well after dark, then I think we need to get clear of here, cross the river, and get into the hills yonder. I shot a buck and he's layin' near the brush. I couldn't get to him but maybe we can pick him up as we cross. I just hope they don't find him. If they do, they'll start lookin' for us and that won't be none too good," explained Tate.

"I'm glad you didn't start a fire," he said, but was interrupted by a grinning Maggie.

"Well, we weren't too sure the great big hunter would bring home any meat!"

He looked at the redhead and responded, "Well, I could do

like the Comanche do and make you go get the meat, you know, dress it out, skin it, cut it up and cook it. But, well, you know, I just didn't wanna see that pretty red hair hangin' from some warrior's scalp lance."

Maggie laughed and playfully slapped Tate's shoulder and turned to the packs to retrieve their cold rations for supper. It would be a cold camp, no coffee, just pemmican and water, but no one complained.

Before they moved out, Tate did a re-check of all their gear to make sure there were no noise makers. Satisfied, he swung aboard Shady and looked at the star lit sky with the wide band of the Milky Way arching above. The moon was waning past half and gave little light. It was only their night-time accustomed vision that aided their way as Tate led the small entourage from the ravine. He paused at the mouth of the ravine, stepped down and with Lobo at his side, climbed atop the lip of the gulch to survey the distant camp. The glow of low burning fires marked the site and also told of the raiding party's lack of concern about being seen.

Tate slid from the slope, stepped into his stirrup and motioned for the women to follow. He led the packhorse and rode directly to the break in the trees where the deer took their water. Once in the break, they were obscured from the Indian encampment and Tate stepped down. He quickly field-dressed the deer, threw the heart to Lobo, and left the entrails, head and legs behind. He secured the carcass atop the packhorse. He walked to the water's edge, saw the starlight reflecting from the ripples and said, "Looks like a good crossing, don't appear too deep. I'll lead the way, don't follow too close and watch what my horse does. If you see him drop down and start swimming, then hold on tight and let your horse have her head. If you start to lose your seat, slip off on the downstream side and hold on, your horse will pull you along and you'll be alright. Got that?"

Maggie nodded her head and said, "Yes, I'll be fine. I'll just trust my horse."

Tate looked to Singing Bird and with signs asked if she would be alright. She nodded and pointed for him to lead the way. The crossing went without incident, but once across, Maggie was startled when her horse started his rolling shake and she let out a short yelp. Tate swiveled his head around and looked sternly at the woman who held her hand out to the side, palms up to signify she was sorry. Tate motioned for them to lead out and they wasted little time putting the river behind them. Tate brought up the rear, stopping often to search for any sign or sound of pursuit, but was pleased when they made the trees in the foothills and were well away from the river and the raiding party.

With little moonlight, Tate chose to make camp in the dry creek bottom that led from the foothills, believing them to be well out of sight from the encampment below. It was not until they had broken camp and put another five miles behind them that Tate finally stopped to eat.

"I've been thinking about a fresh juicy deer steak ever since we crossed the river," declared Maggie as she speared the steaks cut by Tate. The willow withes would hang the steaks over the small fire and they would soon be ready. In the meantime, Tate was nursing his first cup of coffee and sat comfortably on the sandy creek bottom, leaning against a large piece of driftwood washed up in the last flood. Lobo had trotted off in search of his ration of rabbit and Tate looked over the fire and back the way they had come, to see the distant snow-capped mountain range framed by the nearby juniper covered hills.

"Now, ain't that a pretty sight?" he asked, nodding toward the distant view.

Maggie stopped her work and looked, hands on hips, and

smiled as she said, "Aye, an' I'm beginnin' to understand the pull the mountains had on me father."

"Like 'em do ya'?"

"Ummhummm. I do, that I do."

Singing Bird also looked and pointing, said, "My home."

A FEW WISPY CLOUDS COULD BE SEEN IN THE FAR EAST, hanging just above the timbered hills that marked the edge of the wide park known as Bayou Salado. It would take two to three days to cross this fertile park west to east, and four to five days to cover the grassy plain from south to north. For two days, the travelers had climbed from the Arkansas River valley and now crested the long timbered ridge to take in the panoramic vista. Stretching off to their left and pointing like a white jointed spine lay the string of mountains that towered above timberline showing their naked crags to the blue sky and framing the west boundary of the park. Across the park and marching from the far north to the southernmost portion of the wide plain were lower timber-clad mountains that appeared as dark green blanketed graves of giants of old. A patchwork of rolling hills and grassy slopes dotted with random clusters of juniper and piñon connected to the eastern edge of the park and joined with those where Tate and company now stood.

The entire park appeared as an elongated triangle of grassy plain, rich in game with vast herds of buffalo, deer and antelope, and streams loaded with fish and beaver. The surrounding mountains harbored abundant numbers of grizzly, black bear, elk, bighorn sheep, wolves, coyotes, and more. It also held hot springs, salt springs and salt deposits used by both man and beast. Long claimed by the Ute people, the park had often been the site of battles between tribes trying to wrest control of this rich resource from the Ute. Cheyenne, Arapaho, Comanche, and Sioux had repeatedly come to this valley on hunting and raiding expeditions, leaving behind many of their warriors in those battles for dominance.

An excited Singing Bird was pointing and talking in her Shoshonean tongue mixed with newly learned words in English. Tate and Maggie listened and tried to understand, deciphering words like 'home, people, hunt, buffalo,' and others. It was their hope to find the encampment of the Yamparika Ute and return Singing Bird to her people. She had said her people summered in this park and she could take them to the usual site of their encampment.

"Well, there's till plenty of daylight, so we might as well push on. Don't know if we'll find her people today or not. This is a mighty big park. When I came 'crost it in the spring it took me most o' four days to get from one end to the other. Course, that was cuttin' straight acrost' it too," explained Tate as he gigged his horse forward. He motioned for Lobo to scout ahead and nodded to Singing Bird to take the lead.

"You came this way in the spring when you came to Bent's Fort?" asked Maggie as she rode beside Tate.

"Yes'm."

"So, you live near here?" she inquired.

Tate chuckled and said, "No m'am. My cabin is, oh, I dunno, 'bout two weeks travel, or more, on farther north of here."

Maggie leaned back and looked at Tate quizzically, "You mean you came that far just because Kit Carson asked you?"

"Yes'm. When ol' Beckwourth came knockin' on muh door an' said Kit wanted to see me and he had a job for me, well, it came at just the right time. I didn't have nuthin' else to do an' I had me a case of wanderlust buildin' so, I just packed up an' headed out."

Maggie looked at the grinning face of Tate, shook her head in wonder and turned her eyes away. Every so often she would look at him again, shake her head, and then look over the countryside and a glassy eyed stare would betray her journey into deep thought. She had never encountered anyone the like of these men of the wilderness. The thought that someone would travel for two weeks on nothing more than the word of another was more than she had ever imagined possible. The people she worked with in the Choteau warehouse and other places would hardly cross the road to lend a hand to someone in need and now this man had traveled across country to help someone almost on a whim. She was having a hard time wrapping her mind around such a magnanimous gesture, especially from one so young as Tate.

Suddenly Singing Bird shouted and pointed. Tate immediately saw the cause of her excitement; a thin wisp of smoke spiraled skyward just beyond the timbered shoulder of the nearby mountain. Bird turned back to Tate, grinning broadly, and pointed again repeatedly saying, "My people! My people!" She nudged her appaloosa to a trot, motioning for Tate and Maggie to hurry up.

"Hold on! Hold on little one! We can't go rushin' into their village." He motioned with his hands, flat and pushing down, to slow down.

Bird reined up, nodding her head and chattering, "I am excited to see my family. My mother's father and mother, and my father's brothers are there." But Tate and Maggie couldn't understand everything she said, but her motions, signs, and a few understood words helped them to get the gist of what she intended.

Tate looked to Maggie and said, "We'll just have to let her take the lead. Hopefully, somebody'll recognize her. I don't know how long it's been since her little band left this bunch, but I think we're about to find out."

As they rounded the point of the timbered knob, a wide valley lay between two tree covered hills and pushed back toward the taller mountain range. A stream flowed from the valley and the horses easily crossed the shallow but swift running creek. Nestled in the hollow of the hills was a village of over a hundred hide lodges. Cookfires for the evening meal were scattered throughout the village. A horse herd of several hundred animals grazed in the tall grass nearer the timbered hillock that looked like the hump of a massive buffalo. It was a tranquil scene with the many women busy at the cookfires, children running about chasing one another, and men busy crafting their tools and weapons for hunting.

Tate saw a trio of mounted warriors brandishing lances race from the trees by the black hill, shouting taunts and war-cries, as they neared the intruders. The warriors pulled up in front of Singing Bird and were quickly admonished by the girl as she chattered in the Ute language, motioning to Tate and Maggie, and then to the camp. The apparent leader of the sentries grunted and motioned with his lance, turned to lead the way into the camp. As they neared, Maggie and Tate riding side by side, they heard many exclamations, and what sounded like questions, as the people gathered to see the visitors. They were led through the scattered tipis to the center of the encampment and before a large and decorated tipi. It was obvious this was the lodge of their leader and the escort stopped, motioned for Bird, Tate and Maggie to get down.

Bird stood in front of Tate and Maggie as they waited. The escort had ridden away, leaving them standing in front of their horses as several of the villagers neared. The entry flap of the big lodge was thrown back and the chief stepped out, followed by his woman. Tate could see the excitement in Bird as she recognized the man before her. The giddy girl bounced on her toes as she said, "Grandfather! Grandmother!" The man showed no emotion, but the woman beside him smiled broadly, spread her arms wide and motioned for the girl to come to her. Bird ran to the arms of the short buxom woman and the two hugged one another tightly, talking all the time.

Tate and Maggie were startled when a voice came from behind them, translating all that was being said. "The girl has greeted the mother and father of her mother. The old woman, White Stone Woman, and the chief, Lame Buffalo, are her grandmother and grandfather. Singing Bird is a favored child."

Tate turned to see a middle-aged woman of the people who translated. "I am called Little Otter, I learned your language from my husband who is no longer with us. He was a trapper with the American Fur Company."

"I am called Longbow. This is Margarite or Maggie of the Irish," said Tate, by way of introductions. "Singing Bird's band was slaughtered by a group of white men, outlaws, and we found her. She is the only one that lived," explained Tate.

Little Otter stepped forward and translated for Lame Buffalo and his woman. Singing Bird stayed beside her grandmother and waited until Little Otter had finished speaking. Then the girl added more to the story, motioning toward Tate and Maggie, apparently explaining their rescue. Lame Buffalo looked from his granddaughter to Little Otter and said, "You will be our guests. We will have a lodge and food for you. You must stay with us so we can give kindness for kindness."

When Little Otter finished her translation, Tate nodded and using sign language, said they were grateful and would very much like to stay with Lame Buffalo's people for a while, but they would need to continue their search for Maggie's father. Lame Buffalo nodded, turned to his woman and motioned for her to tend to their granddaughter. Little Otter touched Tate on the arm, "Follow me, I will take you to your lodge."

CHAPTER NINETEEN
LEARNING

"There's gotta be eight, ten, twelve creeks and rivers that flow down into the park, so I think it's a good thing we can stay here and scout out a few each day. Seein' as how your Pa said in his letters he was gonna come to the park here and look for beaver and gold, there's a lot o' country to cover. It'll be kinda nice havin' a warm lodge to come back to, don'tcha think?" asked Tate as he dropped their packs against the back wall of the tipi. Lame Buffalo had given them one lodge, thinking nothing about the two of them sharing the same lodge. Among the Ute, it was not considered taboo for a man and a woman to share a lodge, even if they were not joined in a traditional way. But neither was it assumed the two would act in an inappropriate manner. Both Maggie and Tate were relieved to learn that Little Otter and Singing Bird would also share their lodge.

Maggie was rolling out the bedrolls when Tate spoke, and she replied, "Well, I think you're right. Me father could be most anywhere 'bouts, an' his last letter, at least the last one we received, said nothing about going elsewhere. So, I be agreein' wit' you that it'd be good to have a good look about."

Little Otter, followed by Singing Bird, came through the entry, chattering over her shoulder with the young woman. When she entered, she stopped and looked around as if inspecting the layout of their gear. She smiled and motioned to the bedrolls and said, "It is good that we women are together. We will have time to talk."

"Yes, I agree. And I would like to learn more of your language. Bird was helping me and I would like to learn more. Would you be willing to teach me?" asked Maggie, addressing Little Otter.

"Yes, it would please me to teach you. But to learn our language, you must also learn many of our customs to fully understand," answered Little Otter.

"Oh, that would be wonderful. But for right now, will you help me prepare a cookfire? It's been a long day and we are all rather hungry."

Tate had dropped the pack with the cooking gear, the parfleche with the smoked meat, and the remaining hind quarter of the deer, beside the tipi to the left of the entry. As the women exited the lodge, Tate followed, explaining, "Well, while you ladies take care of supper, I'll take care of the horses. I'm takin' 'em down to the stream and give 'em a good rubdown. They'll get a chance to graze a mite and then I'll either put 'em in with the herd, or I'll hobble 'em. So, I'll be back in a bit."

The women were too busy with their task to pay any attention to Tate, so he wandered off, mumbling to himself something about women and not understanding. The rest of the village paid him no mind as he led the horses away, although a few would sneak a look at the white man, for it was unusual for an intruder like this to be among them. Especially at this time of year when many preparations had to be made and the most sacred time was soon approaching.

IT WAS the dim light of early morning when Tate swung aboard Shady and with Lobo at the side, he retraced their steps of the day before. When given the choice of staying in camp with Little Otter and Singing Bird or getting back in the saddle to ride the creeks with Tate, Maggie opted for a time of learning customs and language. In the park, they had crossed three creeks on their way to the village and Tate wanted to check out each one. With the last word from Maggie's Pa telling of his intent to trap and pan the creeks and rivers of the park, he knew they would have to explore each one for any sign of the big Irishman's visit.

Salt Creek, the first stream they crossed, flowed east into the park leaving deposits of salt that many animals and people traveled to find. As the stream slowed in its descent, hampered in its flow by several beaver ponds, the backwater would leave deposits of the much sought-after salt. Tate turned to the west as he followed the meandering stream toward the timber and the distant peaks to begin his search for sign of the Irishman.

Having already seen a couple of O'Shaunessey's camps and diggings, Tate had a pretty good idea what to look for that would tell of the man's passing. Most white men are much more careless in their camp keeping than are the natives who try to live in harmony with the land and prefer to leave no sign of their passing, but the white men want to leave their mark, intentionally or otherwise, wherever they pass. And Michael Patrick O'Shaunessey was no different. When he searched for gold, there were signs of digging along the streams which made Tate think the man had a rocker box to wash the gravel in his search for color. And when he dug prospect holes near the timberline away from the streams, he would usually dig straight into the mountain. And his shelters or lean-tos, by necessity, were larger than most to accommodate the size of the man.

Tate was thorough in his search but found nothing on Salt Creek, nor on the next two unnamed streams that came from the higher mountains. But when he came from the last stream, he was surprised to see a small herd of antelope, causing him to take bow in hand and start a stalk through a dry gulch and take a nice sized doe. The women were pleased with the fresh meat but Maggie said, "It's so small. You didn't shoot a baby, did you?"

Tate chuckled and said, "Look at the hide, see the difference? That's an antelope. They're smaller, but you might like the change from deer meat." He spoke over his shoulder as he led Shady to water and graze. Lobo chose to stay with the women, anticipating some scraps from their butchering of the meat, and he wasn't disappointed.

"I TAKE it by your silence that you didn't find any sign of me father today?" asked Maggie. Tate was sitting on a log, nursing his coffee. Supper was over, and they were enjoying the quiet of the evening. The constant chatter of the three women had slowed to be interspersed with moments of contemplation.

"No, no sign. Just lot's of pretty country. So, did you learn a lot today?" asked Tate.

"Oh yes, and we have something exciting to tell you. But I'll let Bird and Otter tell you."

"Uh, alright then. I'm listenin'," responded Tate, a little hesitant to hear whatever had them so excited. Usually something of that manner meant more work for him, but he was game.

"The Sun Dance of my people will be soon, and I will be in it, and I want you to stay," began Singing Bird. She had carefully practiced the words in English and was excited about speaking them to Tate. She grinned broadly then motioned to Little Otter to tell the rest.

"The Sun Dance is the most sacred of our people's ceremonies. It is a time when young people commit themselves to be a part of our people and to become one with the Great Spirit. Young men must seek the leading of the Spirit before being a part and then there is much to do. Singing Bird believes the Spirit led her during her time alone after her people crossed over, and she has been chosen to follow the medicine way."

Tate looked at Singing Bird who sat with her head down and not looking at anyone. He asked her, "The medicine way? Are you sure?"

Bird looked up at her friend and nodding her head, replied, "Yes. My father was our Shaman and we spoke of it before. I believe this is what I must do."

Little Otter continued, "The dance is for four days, but the time before the dance, and during the dance, there is much required and expected of the family. Singing Bird would like for you and Morning Sky to be her family during this time."

Tate did a double take and asked, "Morning Sky?"

All three of the women smiled and laughed as Maggie answered, "Yes, Longbow, that is the name I have been given because of my red hair. I am to be called Morning Sky, isn't it wonderful?"

Tate lifted his eyebrows as he looked at the redhead and chuckled, "I leave you for one day and you've already turned Indian on me. I just can't leave you alone, can I?" He shook his head, grinning, and looked to Otter and said, "Go ahead, tell me more."

"There will be others, other bands of the Yamparika, maybe some bands from the Mouache and White River, perhaps others. When the circle is built, this lodge will be moved to be near the circle and you will need to pray and support her."

"Alright, we can do that," replied Tate, nodding and looking at Maggie who agreed.

"There will be other things, but I will tell you those as the time is closer."

Tate looked to Singing Bird and said, "This is a special time for you. I know these things are usually done just by young men, and for you to do this is very special and difficult too. We will be with you all the time. You make us very proud."

When Otter finished translating, Bird looked to both Tate and Maggie and said, "I am grateful to you. I have come to look to you as my family and this makes me very happy."

Maggie quickly wrapped the girl in a tight hug and the two shed a few tears together. Tate smiled at these two women that had worked their way into his heart and he wondered what the future would hold. In the meantime, he had a lot of country to search and for now, his bedroll seemed to be calling his name.

CHAPTER TWENTY
CLAIM

Tate, Lobo and Shady had explored the valleys, draws and canyons of several creeks that led into the park, all to no avail. He did however, take game on every outing and the bounty was shared with many of the folks in the village. Little Otter had become quite popular with her many gifts of fresh meat and Maggie had always accompanied her on these forays. Tate was starting on another explorative venture and was packing his gear for the day's journey, when Maggie approached, "May I join you?"

"Well, of course. You're always welcome, but today's journey might be a bit long," he explained, "I've already checked the valleys nearby, so it'll take more time to get to where we need to go today."

"That's alright. Litter Otter has some duties today and I think a change of scenery would do me good," she rested her hand on the withers of Shady as she looked at Tate, "Besides, we haven't ridden together for several days now, and Lobo asked me to come today." She grinned at Tate, looked down at Lobo who came to his feet beside Maggie, pushed against her for some petting, and with mouth open and tongue lolling, he looked at Tate as if to agree with the woman.

DEAR MARIA,

Bayou Salado is like paradise. There are so many animals, deer, elk, antelope, and the creeks and rivers are full of beaver. The mountains all around are beautiful and this park is magnificent! I have trapped many beaver, some otter, and even some mink. Also, I have found color in some of the streams, not a lot, but enough to show there is gold here. I believe I will spend the winter here, trapping is always best in the early spring when the snow melts and the beaver coats are prime. I will spend this fall looking for more gold and, God willing, next summer I can come for you and Margarite.

You will love this country, my Maria, the mountains are beautiful, the forests are so thick they appear almost black. The park is green with grass and where the streams run, there are cottonwoods, willows, and much game. There are some natives, but we leave each other alone and they have been no bother. We could live very well in this country. I might even find a place to start to build a cabin for us. I am anxious to see you and Margarite again. Don't ever forget that I love you both.

Your loving husband,

Daniel Patrick O'Shaunessy

"I DID FIND ONE CABIN, but I'm sure it wasn't built by your father. It's been there at least a couple of years and the doorway was too low, even for me. Your father wouldn't have built one that he had to crawl into!" explained Tate as the two rode north. They were bound for where the South Platte River came from the mountains, and with the larger stream and wider valley, they were hopeful of finding some sign of Maggie's father. "And this was the last letter you got from him?" he asked as he waved the letter towards her.

"Aye, it came in last winter, just before me mother died. It pleased her to hear him say he wanted to see us, but she was too weak even to get her hopes up."

"Well, if he spent this last winter in the park, he might still be here. But if he had a good harvest of plews, he might have taken off to the tradin' post to cash 'em in and resupply. Now, the way I figger it is, if he found gold and plenty of beaver, even if he did leave, he'll come back. We just need to check every valley and creek and maybe we'll find his cabin, or some other sign."

His comments went unanswered by Maggie as she lapsed into her own thoughts about her father. She remembered him as a big lovable man, always gentle with her, kind and loving to her mum. They had a good family life, but he was always wanting to see what was on the other side of the hill, always wanting more for his family. A hard worker, he never lacked for work, but without a proven trade or education, he thought he was never able to do enough for his family. After he went west, it was difficult for Maggie and her mother, but Maggie was able to work and provide enough for them to get by, but her mum had taken ill all too soon. The young woman was at a loss as what to do, believing her mum was suffering as much from a broken heart as from consumption, but Maggie worked hard and did all she could. Now she was determined to find her father, but lately she was a little confused as to whether she wanted to find him because she loved and missed him, or because she was angry with him.

"This'll prob'ly be the last valley we can check 'fore we have to move on, it's a little far from the village. An' with the Sun Dance startin' soon, we'll need to stay there with Singing Bird," remarked Tate, filling the quiet time with words.

Maggie lifted from her reverie and said, "You're right. Little Otter said the Dance lasts for four days, but we'll need some time before to move the lodge and spend time with Bird."

"Hey! Lookee there!" Tate was standing in his stirrups pointing to a junction of a stream coming from the mountains to their left and the river beside them.

Maggie didn't see what he was pointing at and asked, "What? What do you see?"

"There, by the stream comin' from up yonder, those are diggin's. Somebody's been prospectin' there." He nudged his horse forward to the site, slipped from the saddle and started investigating the location. Maggie was soon at his side, the horses were drinking from the stream, and Lobo took off after a rabbit. Tate pushed at a small pile of gravel with his foot, and pointing, said, "See there, that's were a rocker box sat, and he was diggin' from the gravel in the stream and here on the bank. Even looks like he moved them rocks out there in the stream, see how they're piled up right there, that ain't natural. Yeah, whoever it was, spent a little time here. Musta found somethin' to keep him around." Something caught his eye in the riffle beside a stone, he bent down and brought up a handful of wet gravel, swished it around in his palm and with his other hand, plucked out a stone. He held it up to Maggie, "And this is what done it!" He held a small nugget, about the size of his little fingernail, to show Maggie what had drawn her father to the west.

"Ohhh, that's a gold nugget? What's it worth?" asked the redhead.

"Ahh, it's a little one, so it ain't worth much, maybe twenty, twenty-five dollars," answered a sober faced Tate.

"Twenty-five dollars? That little thing? And you just picked it outta the water?" exclaimed an excited Maggie. She looked at the stream, expecting to see gold everywhere. She reached into the water and brought up a handful of gravel, pushed her fingers through it, searching, but was disappointed. She looked up at Tate and said, "How come I didn't find one?"

"That's what prospectin's all about. A man could move every rock in this stream and never find another one, and then again, he might find a bushel of 'em. Ya' just never know."

Tate chuckled at the woman and began looking around searching for something. At the edge of a cluster of willows that overhung the creek, he saw what he was looking for, a pile of rock. Maggie watched as he walked to the small stack of stones and began removing them, one at a time. He found what he wanted and walked back to Maggie, holding out his hand.

She looked at his grinning face, down to his stretched-out hand, and saw a familiar coin. "Is it? Is it a farthing?" She reached out and took the coin, bridling her excitement for just a moment, then looked back at Tate. "It is! Me father was the one digging here! This is his claim! And there is gold here! Oh, Tate, this is wonderful!"

"Now, don't go gettin' too excited, we've seen things like this before."

"I know, I know, but surely he found some gold? You did. And since he found gold, that means he'll be back," she pleaded, searching for some hope to hang onto, anything.

"Ummhumm, and look upstream there, those are beaver dams. So, he prob'ly found some beaver too. So, yes, it seems to be a place he'll come back to, so, how 'bout we have us a bit to eat and we'll head back to the village."

It was just after the sunset colors faded from the west when Tate and Maggie rode back into the village. An anxious Singing Bird greeted them as they arrived at the lodge, "I was beginning to worry about you," she explained, using her newly learned English, proudly. "Tomorrow is the beginning of days for the Sun Dance and there is much to do." Maggie put her arm around the girl and walked with her into the lodge, enjoying the role of substitute mother.

With several other bands joining Lame Buffalo's village for the Sun Dance, the valley of the Black Mountain had become crowded with lodges and horse herds. The brush arbor for the Sun Dance had been erected near the mouth of the valley, apart from the populous village. Several tipis of the families of the dancers surrounded the circular site, near enough to give support to their family member.

"The purification ceremony in the sweat lodge is the beginning of the dancer's duties. The tradition is called *taguwuni* or Standing Thirsty and the dancers do this for themselves, their families, and their people." Little Otter was standing beside Maggie and Tate and explaining the steps of the traditional Sun Dance. Lame Buffalo and White Stone Woman, as the grandparents and family of Singing Bird, stood nearby. "They will now go to their families to prepare for the dance." Little Otter touched Maggie for her to follow and together with White Stone Woman, they ducked into the tipi that sat just away from the dance circle.

Tate had watched as the circle was prepared and now admired the handiwork of the people. In the center stood a tall cottonwood post, with a fork at the top that held the rafter poles that extended to the outer circle of twelve evenly spaced posts. If one could see it from above, the structure would resemble a wagon wheel. An elk hide had been placed next to the central post and hot coals were brought to the center and sage incense placed upon the coals. The shaman of the village, White Buffalo Horn, shuffled into the center, chanting lowly. He seated himself on the elk-hide, motioned for Lame Buffalo to join him, and the shaman offered the chief the sacred pipe. Lame Buffalo lifted the pipe to the four directions, to the sky and to the earth, then drew deeply of the smoke, and let it out slowly. The shaman repeated the action, and both men lifted their hands heavenward and muttered a soft prayer. As the two men stood to leave, the dancers started into the circle.

"Our leaders have offered their prayers to the Great Spirit and now the dance will begin," spoke Little Otter softly, now at the side of Tate with Maggie standing before him. "Each dancer will be tethered to the center pole, which signifies the Great Spirit, and they will dance from the outer ring, which signifies the people of their band, toward the pole."

"How long will they dance?" asked Maggie, quietly.

"The dance will last four days."

Maggie was aghast as she looked at Little Otter and asked, "They dance continuously for four days?"

"Oh no, they will only dance when the drums and singers call them to dance. But it will be for most of each day," explained Otter. "They have sage around their wrists and some around their ankles, and sage is burnt on the coals for purification and as prayers. The dancers will pray continuously while they dance."

"Is there something special they pray for, or should we know?" queried the redhead.

"They seek 'medicine power', for themselves, their families and their people. But what exactly that is, is between them and the Great Spirit," answered Otter.

The drums began, and the singers began chanting, prompting each of the dancers to begin their shuffling and prancing dance from the outer ring to the post and back. It was evident that Singing Bird was the only woman among the dancers by her attire. While the others had leggings, breechcloths, and adornment of feathers, bone breastplates or other beaded accessories, Bird had leggings under her long tunic and her only adornment was a hairpipe choker and tufts of fur in her long braids. Her tunic was split up the sides almost to her waist, and the sleeves barely covered her shoulders, and she carried a feathered fan in each hand.

As they danced, the participants were intent on their moves and their prayers, ignoring the many family members and tribal leaders that watched from outside the circle. Each dancer had a whistle made from the wing bone of an eagle and would use it to emphasize their prayers. As the sun rose overhead, the heat increased, and the rafter poles provided little relief from the blazing orb. After just over two hours of continuous dancing, the drums rose in intensity and the singers' voices increased in volume, to signify the ending of this portion of the dance. The sound stopped suddenly, and the dancers stopped moving, but stood trembling. One family member was allowed to assist the dancer and White Stone Woman did the honors for this first break. She aided Singing Bird to be seated in place, wiped her forehead and neck with a cool damp cloth, and spoke encouragingly to the girl.

Soon the family members had to leave the circle and White Buffalo Horn and two medicine men from the other bands, Snake Eater and Stands Alone, came into the circle. The three Shamans were seated next to the center post and began instructing the dancers regarding their dancing and prayers and the purpose of the dance and their sacrifice. The words of the Shamans were spoken just loud enough for the dancers to hear as the words were not for the families or others.

As the drums called the dancers forth, Little Otter spoke to Tate and Maggie, "There will be other times when they stop, and you can each go to her aid. She cannot have anything to drink or eat until after the dance is complete, but she needs to know you are here and praying for her. I must go, I have other duties."

Tate and Maggie sat upon a blanket, side by side, and watched the dancers and the families around the circle. Some of the supporters had uplifted hands and faced heavenward as they muttered their prayers, and others with heads bowed did the same. Some were chanting prayers along with the drums and singers, but all were actively involved in the dance. Tate clasped Maggie's hand in his and began to pray quietly, but just loud enough for Maggie to hear. He prayed, not just for Singing Bird, but for Bird's quest to become a Shaman of her people. He also prayed for the Ute people, Lame Buffalo and White Stone Woman, and for Maggie and the search for her father. When he finished, he looked to Maggie to see tears rolling down her freckled cheeks and he was prompted to begin singing.

Amazing Grace, how sweet the sound. That saved a wretch like me.

I once was lost, but now I'm found. Was blind, but now I see.

Maggie joined him as he continued,

Thro' many dangers, toils and snares, I have already come;

Tis grace hath bro't me safe thus far, and grace will lead me home.

Lame Buffalo and White Stone Woman watched the two

as they sang, and the music brought a smile to both faces. When they finished, Lame Buffalo, nodded his head and turned back to watch the dancers.

Soon, the drums stopped, and Maggie was motioned forward to help Bird. When she returned, she was shaking her head in wonder at what the dancers were able to do as they continued. As dusk fell, the dancers were given blankets to sleep on until they were called awake to greet each sunrise with prayer and sacred songs. The families returned to their lodges each night but would also greet each sunrise with prayer as they supported their dancers.

By the end of the fourth day, every dancer had collapsed at least once, and now as the dance was ending, several lay collapsed in exhaustion but many continued, among them was the frail figure of Singing Bird. When the volume and intensity of the drumming and singing increased to mark the final phase of the dance, Singing Bird danced to the center post and wrapped her arms around it to stay upright, exhausted as she was, she expressed her love of the Great Spirit in this manner. When the drums ceased, family members assisted each dancer to the sweat lodge for a final brief purification before the dancer was to return to their family.

White Stone Woman and Maggie assisted Singing Bird as she made her way to the lodge. Once inside, she was seated on the bedroll, and Little Otter spoon-fed her a thin broth while White Stone Woman wiped her face and neck. The chief's woman motioned for Tate to leave, and as he stepped from the lodge, Lame Buffalo greeted him and motioned for him to be seated alongside on the grey log. When they realized the women would be busy with their ministrations and Singing Bird, the men helped themselves to a plate full of stew.

Tate was surprised when Lame Buffalo spoke in English, "You have been good for our Singing Bird. You will always be welcome in our village."

Tate sat his plate aside and spoke in both English and sign, "We are grateful we were allowed to be a part of this special time. We are honored by you and your people."

"You search for the father of Morning Sky?" asked Lame Buffalo.

"Yes, we found where he had camped, and some other sign. I believe we might even find him here in Bayou Salado. But it will take time. We must leave soon. The moon when the grass turns brown will come soon and we must find him before then."

"Where you go, if you need help, send word and my people will come," stated the chief.

"I am honored for that, and if I can be of help to you, send word," answered Tate. "Longbow would count it an honor to be of help to my brothers, the Yamparika."

The women flipped the entry cover aside and White Stone Woman led the three from the lodge. Maggie seated herself beside Tate and said, "She is sleeping. I think she will sleep for several days, the poor girl is exhausted. I'm tired just from watching her!"

Lame Buffalo stood beside his woman, "We thank you both for being with Singing Bird. We ask you to come to our lodge before you leave." He nodded and the two walked away. Maggie looked at Tate and asked, "We're leaving?"

"Well, yeah, but I didn't say when, just soon. But the sooner the better."

"I will stay with Singing Bird, you may leave at any time," shared Little Otter.

"Well, we'll decide that come tomorrow. Right now, I think we all need a little sleep," answered Tate as he ran his hand through the scruff of Lobo's neck. The wolf trotted into the lodge, flopping down beside Tate's bedroll as if he was more tired than the others. All he had done for the last four days was run through the woods with several of the village youngsters and maybe they had tired him out a little.

CHAPTER TWENTY-TWO
TROUBLE

THE CAMPFIRE STRETCHED THE SHADOWS OF THE MOUNTAIN muggers to the tops of the ponderosa surrounding the clearing. They had their fill of the fresh venison and sprawled lazily staring into the flames. The mesmerizing flicker of fire had a strange magnetism that drew the campers into its aura and carried them into the realm of reverie. Three men sat glassy-eyed, lost in their own thoughts and memories of both problems and possibilities.

Suddenly the silence was broken by the crackly voice of B.O., "Here's the way I see it. We been follerin' that big mick for four days now, and I'm thinkin' he's headin' back to his diggins. Now, I'm also thinkin' that a couple bags o' gold dust'd be better'n what'ere supplies he might have left."

"But B.O., we lost him that one time. If we lose him agin' we won't get no gold or supplies," whined Dingus.

"But if we hang back fur 'nuff, we can still foller his tracks, an' he won't know we're follerin'. I think he spotted us last time and hid his trail on us. But like I figgered he kept goin' and we found his trail. So, if'n we just hang back fur 'nuff, he won't need to hide his trail an' we can catch up when he gets to his diggins," explained B.O.

"'Sides, Dingus, we got 'nuff supplies to last us, an' if we had us some gold nuggets like he had, we'd have us a high time in Sante Fe!" added Nits.

Dingus looked to Nits, chuckled at the thought of a high time, and added, "Wal, my idee of a high time is all the whiskey I kin drink all to onct. You kin have them barflies, an' the way you smell it'd take a whole bag o' gold to git one o' them to pay attention to yuh."

"Hah! I'll have you know, I was once quite the dandy back in St. Louie! Had me some fancy duds, money, women, whiskey, an' a high-steppin' horse. An' if I had me 'nuff money, I'd show you a thing'r two," countered Nits.

"What? You? I cain't see it. We'd have to put you on a spit an' smoke you o'er the fire to get rid o' them bugs whut took up a home on your filthy hide! Whut'chu got against soap n' water anyway?" asked B.O.

"Nuthin'. Just don't see the need. Yuh wash up, get all clean an' duded up, an' yuh just get dirty all o'er agin," explained Nits as he plucked another hardback from his neckline and popped it between his thumbnails. "Course, I will admit, it were purty nice when I was all decked out and had on that stinkwater, the women found me plum irre-sistible!"

"Whooooeeee! Bout th' onliest thing that'd find you irre-sistible now would be a grizzly, an' he'd have to be starvin' at that!" declared Dingus. He turned his attention to B.O. and asked, "You still think that big mick is headed to Bayou Salado?"

"Wal, he's sure headed in the right direction, an' it's good country, that's fer sure. We'll prob'ly get there in a couple days. Course we don't know where his diggins are, but we'll just wait n' see."

"Wal, you'ns can talk all you want. Me, I'm gettin' me some shuteye!" proclaimed Nits, walking to his bedroll. The three bedrolls were arrayed around the campfire, placing each man within the circle of warmth from the dying flames. By midnight, the coals gave little heat and less light as the whisper of smoke drifted toward the stars.

The pack mule was the first to sense danger and began nervously side stepping, bumping into the horses on either side. The horses' ears pricked forward, nostrils flared, and eyes widened as the low rumble of stifled whinnies came from deep in their chests. With three horses and one mule tethered to the picket line, their nervous prancing and snuffling wakened the three men. They rolled from their blankets, rifles in hand as they tried to pierce the darkness to see the cause of alarm.

Suddenly, the panicked bray of the mule startled man and beast alike as a thundering roar came from behind the animals. The blackness of a moonless night and the dense cover of thick pines hid the charging grizzly from their sight. When the bear stood on his hind legs, he towered over the horses and with fangs bared, he roared as he lunged on the hind quarters of the nearest horse. He buried his long claws into the haunches of the horse and sunk his teeth deep in the meaty rump. The panicked horse kicked back, catching the beast in the groin and gut, but the bear didn't release his grip. The horse tried to run forward, but the picket line momentarily stopped him. The other horses and mule also pushed against the picket line strung between the two trees, and it suddenly snapped.

When the horses and mule lunged forward, the men had to dive for cover to escape the charge that scattered the bedrolls and coals of the fire. The horse with the grizzly continued to kick at its attacker and fought to get away and follow the others. The bear still growled and dug his claws deeper as it sought to bring his prey to the ground. The rear legs of the horse gave way and the terrified animal futilely dug with his front legs to try to escape, screaming in frightened agony.

Once the other horses had fled, the men saw the attacking beast and one after another, took aim and fired at the grizzly. The old silver-tip boar released his grip on the horse and rose to stand tall on his hind legs to face the new threat of the men. Frantically the three were reloading and watching the beast. When the bear dropped to all fours and charged, B.O. and Nits panicked and ran. Dingus quickly finished reloading and gave chase. The fleeing men had cleared the timber and were running into the grassy flats, the lumbering grizz barking his growl, was gaining. Suddenly the bear caught up with Nits and without slowing, swatted the man aside and continued after B.O. Dingus ran for all he was worth and saw B.O. stumble and fall headlong in the grass. Just as the grizzly rose to his full height to stand over the fallen man, Dingus dropped to a seated position and took aim. He squeezed off his shot and a puff of dust rose from the chest of the grizzly, barely seen in the starlight, and the bear staggered backwards, and fell unmoving.

B.O. jumped to his feet, still holding his rifle, and hurriedly finished reloading. Slowly, he approached the downed beast, rifle at the ready, and seeing no movement, poked the bear in the side with the muzzle of his rifle. The bear did not respond. B.O. stepped back, breathed deeply, and looked around for his partners. Dingus was walking towards him, reloading and the crumpled form of Nits could be seen back away from the dead bear.

B.O. and Dingus walked to the still body of Nits, "See, even the grizz couldn't stand the smell of 'im. He just smacked him down and kept comin' after me," proclaimed

B.O. Dingus rolled the man over and both men stepped back at the sight of the ripped open side with guts spilling out. The four-inch claws of the grizzly had opened up Nits from shoulder to hip. "He was dead 'fore he hit the ground," exclaimed the big B.O., "that grizz was a mean'un."

It was early afternoon on the following day before the two men were back on the move. They didn't bother burying their friend and after spending much of the morning skinning the grizzly, then fighting with the horses and the mule to try and load the hide, they gave up and kept only the claws. The horses were too frightened of the smell of the beast to let the men near as they packed the hide. The mule switched ends and tried unsuccessfully to kick some sense into the two men. Finally, the two decided that although the hide would bring a good price at the traders, the fight with the frightened horses wasn't worth the effort. When they gave up on the task, the skittish animals let them approach and after several tries, they were able to get mounted and on the way.

"So, are we still gonna go fer that Irishman's gold?" asked Dingus.

"You got'ny better idees?" answered B.O.

"Nope, suits me. It looks like that feller is headin' straight into that notch yonder. The one to the right of that high peak. Looks like it goes through a purty narrow canyon," observed Dingus, pointing to the south. "Shore hope he knows where he's a goin'," drawled Dingus.

"Wal, you just keep us on his trail, but 'member, don't get too close. We don' wan' 'im coverin' his sign agin. Wastes too much time havin' to back track. But as I look at these hyar mountains, he coulda got his gold just 'bout anywheres," observed the big man.

"I think yore right 'bout him headin' to the Bayou Salado.

Cuz he had a good load o' pelts with him, if you recomember. An' I ain't seen too many places in these high up mountains, whut's good fer beaver. Yup, I'd bet on Bayou Salado," answered Dingus, talking as much to himself as to B.O.

CHAPTER TWENTY-THREE
TIMBERLINE

"So, Maccabee, do ye think we lost 'em?" The big Irishman had taken to talking to his dapple-grey gelding some time ago, and he found him to be good company. He always listened, often agreeing by shaking his head up and down, never talking back and in general just being a patient friend. Daniel leaned down and patted the big horse on the side of his neck, speaking softly in his ear. "But ya know, boy. I'ma thinkin' we need to take the high road, so we kin see if any o' them blokes is still followin', aye, that's what we be doin'." He sat upright on the long-legged horse. The big grey stood just over sixteen hands with a broad chest, rump and well-muscles throughout. He had shown himself to be a one-man horse and had proven to be a bit hostile toward any others that approached or dared to touch him by baring his teeth and taking a chunk out of any nearby creature. He barely tolerated the bay packhorse, and made the animal keep his distance.

Daniel came from the steep sided valley and pointed his horse toward timberline on the long bald ridge that towered over the valley. The zig-zag trail made several switchbacks on the long climb out of the valley and the bright sun of early afternoon was welcome when they broke from the trees into the open. A smattering of bristle-cone pines pointed their blushing branches to the south-west in response to the ever-present wind at the high elevations.

As he reached the crest of the first bald knob, Daniel reined up and took in the unbelievable panorama. To the east, the mountains quickly fell away to hold the prairie on the fingertips of the foothills and the flatlands disappeared in the distance. Behind him to the north the long spine of granite peaks stretched away into the grey mist of the high altitude. To the west the Creator had lined out a collection of bare top peaks that appeared as handfuls of carefully fash-ioned clusters decorated with whipped icing. And through the wide gap directly to his south, he saw the familiar broad park of the Bayou Salado.

He had already begun to think of the park as home, hoping to make a more permanent home and build a cabin in the foothills overlooking the park. He stepped down and stood in front of the gelding, soaking in the beauty of the mountainous terrain and the green valley beyond. He turned back and rubbing his fingers on the face of the horse, "Mac-cabee, that be home, sure enough. It's that feelin' I get right here," patting his own chest, "do ye feel it too, boy?" The horse tossed his head up and down, liking the scratching on his face but making O'Shaunessy think he was answering him. "I knew it! Ye feel it too, don't ye?"

Timberline is that point or line beyond which timber will not grow. Partly due to the altitude, also because the snow is held at those altitudes well into the summer months. The scarcity of good soil is due to wind and snow-melt carrying the good soil below, leaving behind granite and limestone slab rock and hard packed gravel. With nothing growing but ground hugging lichen and similar plants, it appears as a barren and uninhabitable land.

Daniel chose to walk and lead the horses, carefully picking his route and avoiding the unstable slide rock as much as possible. It was not the safest place to travel, but with no cover for man or beast, Daniel knew he could see if anyone was in pursuit as far back as three miles, if anyone dared to follow. Before he got anywhere near his diggings, he wanted some assurance there was no one behind him. This was the fifth day after leaving the trading post at Fort St. Vrain and he had two to three days of travel before him to reach his homesite, and he wanted both his homesite and his claim to be unknown to anyone but him.

They dropped from the bald ridge into a hollow with a dry creek bed in the bottom. Another switchback game trail led them to the top of the next bald mountain that joined with the last peak before he was to drop to the valley floor. It was against his usual practice to ride the ridge-top and skyline himself to anyone below, but he knew they were high enough that if anyone did see them, they would have a hard time making out if they were Indian or white man or a couple of grizzlies. By late afternoon, they crested the last peak, paused for a brief rest and another scan of the panoramic view. Satisfied that no one was following, Daniel was relieved, but was breathing hard; the altitude was tough on anyone that wasn't accustomed to this altitude, and he was anxious to get off the mountain and find a suitable camp in the aspen below.

Suddenly a marmot whistled, startling the horses who jerked back on the leads, causing Daniel to fall backwards and hit his head on one of the granite slabs. The horses didn't go but a couple steps backward, and Maccabee dropped his head to sniff at the red-bearded man at his feet. The gelding snorted, blowing snot on the face of Daniel and bringing him around. The man struggled to sit up and wipe his face with the sleeve of his capote as he looked up at the curious face of Maccabec. "Thanks!" he said, but the movement made him grab at the knot at the back of his head and let out a moan. He struggled to stand and realized he had caught his foot between two stones and twisted his ankle which was already swelling. When he tried to put his weight on it, he started to fall but caught the mane of Maccabee. "Aye, tis a fine fix that we are in now, me bucko, but a good laugh and a long sleep are the two best cures. Now let's see 'bout gettin' off this mountain."

He walked alongside the big grey, using the saddle horn for support as he hobbled along. They found a game trail that seemed to drop away from the peak, probably used by bighorn sheep at some time in the past. Once in the trees, Daniel stopped the horses, fought his way to the uphill side, and after several painful tries, managed to get mounted. Once atop, they made good progress and soon found a good clearing between some black timber and a sizable grove of aspen. A small spring fed creek seeped from the rocks and patches of grass promised graze for the horses.

Once aground, Daniel crawled to the aspen, cut a forked sapling to fashion into a crutch, scooped out a small pool for the ice-cold water and soaked his ankle until he no longer had feeling in it. A small fire accorded enough flame for his coffee and he warmed some smoked meat on a fireside stone for his supper. With the horses tethered, fire banked, and well wrapped in his blankets, Daniel settled in for a well-deserved and much needed night's rest. Tomorrow, if able, he would follow the river to the last notch between the mountains that would lead him to Bayou Salado.

After riding most of the day with his leg crooked around his saddle horn to keep his injured ankle up, Daniel was anxious to get to the ground. He reined up at the crest of a short climb, finding a good campsite at the edge the treeline. He looked to the south, "Well, there it is Maccabee! Bayou Salado! Aye 'n she's a sight for sore eyes, dinna ye reckon? I'm thinkin' we might rest up here a bit longer. Me ankle is hurtin' for certain, and I'm also thinkin' you an' the bay could use some rest." Using his crutch to aid him, he slipped from the dapple-grey and dropped to put hobbles on the gelding then the bay. It was a struggle, but he soon had the gear off both horses and gathered some firewood for the night. He hobbled to the edge of the clearing for another long look at the park far below and wondered again at the beauty of the land and the size of the country. Below him and in the distance beyond, he could see more land than he had laid eyes on in all his growing up years. The park stretched for well over fifty miles north and south and thirty miles east and west and was well populated with wild game. Daniel filled his lungs with the fresh mountain air lifting his shoulders and closing his eyes to savor the flavor of freedom. It was a grand land, this wild country, and the first place the big man had truly felt at home.

He thought of his wife and child and the promise he made to bring them west. He hoped he could gather enough gold to provide the stake he would need to bring his family west. As he thought about them, he turned away from the park and went to the big stone slab next to the fire and sat down to write another letter to his loved ones. He looked heavenward and said, "Lord, let it be soon that me'n me family can be together. I sure be missin' 'em, yessir, I do."

CHAPTER TWENTY-FOUR
DELAY

ON THE SOUTHERN SHOULDER OF THE BLACK MOUNTAINS, TATE sat with Lobo beside him, watching the sun paint the morning sky with hues of red and orange. Low lying clouds provided the palette for the Creator's masterpiece that filled Tate's thoughts with wonder. The eastern hills were colored by the reflected light, and the wide plains of the park held the glow. Tate had spent the last half hour talking with his Lord, asking for guidance, protection, and comfort for his friends, the Ute, and his companion Maggie and her father.

Lobo lifted his head, looking below, as Maggie climbed the shoulder of the hill to join Tate. "Doin' some prayin' are ye?" she asked as she approached. She sat down beside him and looked to the east to take in the sunrise.

"Ummmhummm, and how is Morning Sky this fine day?" asked Tate, grinning at the redhead. She had taken to her Indian name and was tickled to hear Tate use it.

"Oh, my, isn't that a beautiful sunrise. And what a view, this valley really is spectacular!" She stood to look at the wide park in the morning gold and the colors of the sunrise touched her face, giving her the same glow.

Tate caught his breath as he looked at her, standing with hands on hips, almost leaning into the morning light. He sucked in a deep breath that lifted his shoulders, and he softly said as he looked at her, "Beautiful."

She kept her eyes on the shadowy eastern hills and the splash of colors across the horizon and said, "Yes, it is beautiful." She turned to look at her friend, sat down beside him and asked, "So, have you decided when we're leaving?"

He picked up a small twig, scratched in the dirt at his feet, and said, "I'm thinkin' maybe today, after we spend a little time with Singing Bird. Or, tomorrow at the latest. What'chu think?"

"I've enjoyed our time with Bird's people, and I've learned a lot. They are fine people, but I'm anxious to find my father. So, aye, let's be 'bout our business." She nodded her head as she finished her statement and looked at the village below. Several families of the visiting bands were busy taking down their lodges, preparing for their return to their own lands. A thin cloud of smoke from the morning cookfires hovered over the village and the herds of horses grazed lazily to the west and south of the lodges. It was a tranquil scene and Maggie thought of the similarities with communities of other people, families with children playing, parents busy with the day's chores, and all sharing similar hopes and dreams. She thought *Good people come in all colors and beliefs.*

They stood together and started down the hill, following Lobo, to return to their lodge and have some coffee and corn cakes. They were greeted by a sleepy-eyed Singing Bird and Little Otter, "Oh, it's a beautiful day!" said Bird.

"Yes, isn't it? And how is our young woman on this day? Still tired?" replied Maggie.

Bird stretched her arms over her head and arched her back and answered, "I am a little sore, but that's all." She smiled as she sat on the log by the rekindled fire. Maggie pushed the coffee pot nearer the flames and slid the frying pan around to add the corn cakes. Bird watched and yawned, stretched again, and looked up at Tate, "What? Why are you looking at me like that?" she signed.

Tate grinned and said, "Last week we had a girl traveling with us, and now we leave a young woman with her people." Little Otter translated, and Bird smiled at the words. "Will you begin your study with the Shaman, White Buffalo Horn?"

"Yes, I have long felt the call to become a medicine woman, and the dance has prepared me, and White Buffalo Horn agrees it is the will of the Great Spirit."

"How long will it take for you to become a Shaman?" asked Maggie.

"There is much to learn, and it will take many summers before I am ready."

"So, will you take the place of White Buffalo Horn for this village?" inquired the curious redhead.

"As the Great Spirit leads, sometimes other villages have a need and I could go or if White Buffalo Horn chooses, I could become the Shaman of this village. A Shaman is the medicine woman and must learn of the different means of healing, the many plants and other things that are cures. But the Shaman is also the spiritual leader and directs the people in things of the Spirit and the decisions of moving, planting, battle and more."

"Will you be able to take a mate?" questioned Maggie, smiling at the thought.

Singing Bird dropped her eyes and lifted her head again, trying to show a sober expression but failing as she said, "Yes, if there is one suitable. There were several at the dance that, how you say, showed promise." The three women laughed together, rocking back and forth in their gaiety, but Tate busied himself with pouring a fresh cup of coffee.

When Bird learned her friends were leaving, the two women went for a walk to spend a few more moments together. As they walked arm in arm, Bird asked, "Are you going to have Tate as your man?"

With a nervous laugh, Maggie answered, "Oh, Bird, that's not the way it is with us. He's just helping me find me father, that's all. But he is a fine man, isn't he?"

Bird stopped, turned to look at Maggie and replied, "He is already your man. You two belong together and you should tell him that. Among our people, the man usually does the courting, he comes around with a small flute and plays music outside the lodge to summon his woman. She comes out with a blanket wrapped around her and listens to the music. If she is pleased, she opens the blanket to bring the man to her to show she accepts him."

"But what does the woman do if the man doesn't come with a flute?" asked the redhead, giggling.

"Every woman knows what to do to appeal to the man. If he does not understand that, then he must be the wrong man. But if the woman still wants him, she will go to him with her blanket to invite him," answered Bird.

"You are wise beyond your years, Bird. I believe you will make a very good Shaman."

As they completed their walk, Bird looked to Maggie, tears in her eyes, and said, "You have been my sister. My heart is heavy that you leave, but I will ask the Great Spirit to bring you back." She looked at Tate who was busy loading the horses with their gear and lifted her voice for him to hear, "You have been like a father to me, Longbow, and Morning Sky has been my sister. You must return to my village. My heart will not accept that you leave forever."

Tate turned to the young woman, spread his arms wide and drew her to him in a tight hug. He whispered to her, "You will always be my child, my friend, and Morning Sky's sister. You will see us again, perhaps even soon. But as we both know, that is up to God, or the Great Spirit as you call Him."

Bird leaned back, still held by Tate, and looked up to the man who had saved her and said, "Go in peace, my friend, and return to us soon." She turned away and went to Maggie, hugged her, and walked away from her friends without looking back.

Maggie wiped the tears from her eyes, snatched up her bedroll, tied it behind the cantle, and said, "Time's a wastin', we best be movin'."

Tate looked at the redhead, smiled as she swung aboard the pinto, and stepped into his stirrup and mounted Shady. He looked down at an excited Lobo, motioned for him to lead out, and they kneed their horses after.

They were moving from the mouth of the valley and rounding the shoulder of the black hill when Maggie reined up and said, "We never said goodbye to Lame Buffalo! He wanted us to come to his lodge!"

Tate grinned and said, "While you were walking with Bird, I went to his lodge and said our goodbyes. He gave us gifts," he turned in his saddle, untied the leather thongs behind the cantle and handed her a bundle of buckskin.

Maggie took it, unfolded it, and held before her a fine, rabbit fur lined, beaded buckskin jacket. She looked back at Tate smiling, "This is beautiful! What'd he give you?"

"One just like it."

"Exactly?"

"Yup. Exactly!"

"Well this'll sure come in handy on those cold evenings in the mountains." She turned and tied it behind her cantle. She looked to Tate and said, "They are special people, aye, an' I'm going to miss them."

It was late afternoon and the shadows of dusk were

settling over the park when the duo came to the valley of the South Platte where they had found the diggings of Maggie's father. They crossed the small river and went to the timber side of a long low ridge that paralleled the Platte. On the north side of the ridge, another small stream trickled from the granite peak to the north west, and they found a good campsite in a grove of aspen.

"So, what do we do now? After we found those diggin's, do you think there'll be more?" asked Maggie as she busied herself at the fire.

"Well, if your father is like most men that look for gold, he won't pass up a chance to find a better hole, or what most of 'em call the motherlode. So, we'll check out any promising stream for any other diggin's, or plenty of beaver, and keep lookin' till we find him. See, the best time for beaver is late fall and early spring when they have their winter growth of pelts. So, that leaves the summer for prospectin'. But I'm thinkin' he went to some tradin' post to cash in and resupply, and will probably be back through here, providin' of course, something bad hasn't happened to him."

"Oh, don't say that! I know it's possible and all that, but I don't like to think about it. But," she dropped her eyes and mumbled, "I know I have to face it."

Tate went to her side and she stood as he opened his arms to her. She willingly stepped into his embrace, laying her head against his chest and putting her arms around him. She felt safe in his arms and knew Singing Bird was probably right. This is where she belonged.

CHAPTER TWENTY-FIVE
SIGN

It was a restless night for Tate and he rolled from his blankets well before dawn. With Lobo at his side, he walked up the timbered slope, looking for a promontory to spend some alone time. Finding a sizable rock outcropping, he settled down with his feet hanging over the edge and leaning back against a rotted stump from a lightning struck tree. Lobo sat beside him, but soon grew a bit restless and after nudging Tate with his nose, he trotted off in search of his breakfast. Tate leaned back, looking at the eastern horizon that was beginning to show as a black line beneath a wide band of grey.

"Lord, is it wrong for me to have feelings for Maggie? I mean, it hasn't been that long since I lost White Fawn, and now here's this woman causin' these feelin's and it seems like I'm bein' unfaithful to her. I know, I know, even she told me to find another woman and give her the same love I gave to White Fawn, but, I wasn't expectin' it to be so soon. An' Maggie's different, I mean, she's not from the mountains an' I know she seems to love the wilderness, but makin' it permanent is somethin' else. It ain't like she'd have a bunch o' other women around, I guess I'm just confused. She sure is purty though, and it felt awful good to hold her last night when she was all upset. Lord, I guess what I'm askin' is for you to either show me, tell me, or at least take away the guilt I feel about not bein' true to White Fawn. Course it ain't that I'm bein' untrue, really. Oh, pshaw! I dunno what I mean. Women, they sure can confuse a fella."

He leaned back to watch the sunrise, his favorite time of the day and a time most often spent with his Lord. Now he just wanted to enjoy the colors since his time with the Lord didn't give him the immediate answer he hoped for, and he needed a few moments of reflection. His mother had a favorite bench that faced the east and that sat under the big oak tree in their yard. Tate remembered standing on his bed to look out his window to see his mother sitting with hands folded in her lap, head bowed and lips moving as she talked with her Lord. Tate was barely big enough to rest his chin on the windowsill as he stood on his bed, watching his Ma. He remembered one morning when she returned to stoke the fire in the cookstove and he had gone into the kitchen in his union suit and asked, "Ma, does God always answer your prayers?"

She chuckled and stood with hands on hips and answered, "Why Mr. Tatum, of course He does! God always answers prayers. Sometimes it's yes, sometimes it's no, and sometimes it's wait a while."

"You mean God talks to you?" asked the youngster.

His Ma went to the cupboard, brought out her Bible and said, "He speaks to us through His word. When we read His word, He will use what we read to speak to our hearts so we'll know what to do."

Upon remembering his mother's words, Tate realized he had been somewhat neglectful with his Bible reading. He didn't even have it with him now, but it was back in the saddlebags. *No wonder I can't hear His answer, I haven't been listening.* He clambered to his feet and started back down the hill to the camp. Still thinking about his Ma, he remembered when she told him about the time she was thinking about marrying Pa and how she looked in the Bible for guidance. The first verse she came to was Romans 1:13 that said, "I would not have you ignorant brethren," and she thought that meant she shouldn't have Pa as her husband. But when she looked further, the verse had nothing to do with husbands, just ignorance. Of course, Pa was a little concerned that she would think of him as ignorant, but they put it behind them and had a good marriage.

Maggie was still in her blankets and Tate stirred up the campfire coals to start a fresh pot of coffee. He had retrieved his Bible from the saddlebags and sat down to await the water boiling and began to randomly thumb through the pages. He stopped in I Corinthians and began to read.

"Whatcha readin'?" asked Maggie as she stood beside him, stretching and yawning.

"Oh, just a little of the Bible," he explained. His eyes had just come to chapter 7 and verse two almost jumped off the page, "*. . . let every man have his own wife and let every woman have her own husband.*" He quickly closed the Bible, fearful she had seen the words, and reached for the coffee pot. He scrambled for the bag of coffee beans, poured some on the flat rock and began crushing them to prepare the coffee. He kept his head ducked and eyes averted, humming mindlessly to himself. He saw Maggie move away to make her way into the trees for her time and he sat back, relieved.

Breakfast was a special treat. Maggie had found some duck eggs and with the last of their pork belly and some cornbread biscuits; it was a mountain man feast. As they sat back enjoying their coffee, Maggie asked, "You look a little pensive this morning, are you alright?"

"Oh yeah, I was just thinkin'. See that ridge yonder?" he pointed to the east at a long timber topped ridge that stretched north and south, cutting the park like a dividing line. "On the other side, there's twice as much country as on this side. Now, if we keep goin' northeast along this here line of mountains, which I believe we should, it's gonna take us, oh, maybe four or five days to do a quick check of the streams an such and get to the north end of the park. Then we can come back south along that far line of hills, although I don't think that country would be too promisin' for gold, but I ain't a prospector neither. Anyway, we can come back south there and maybe even through the middle o' the park to check the streams and such. Only thing is, all that's gonna take us three, four weeks. And we'll be runnin' outta summer purty soon. This is mighty big country and it would be real easy to miss findin' your father. So, I'm thinkin' we'll just do a simple check of each of the streambeds that we come across, go upstream a little way, but not too far, and save us some time. Then when we get to the north end of the park, we'll re-evaluate our plan and decide what to do then. What do you think?"

"Well, I was going to ask you if we could do something like that. I just don't want to get too far away from the diggings we found up that valley back there. I really feel he's going to come back to that spot, and soon. Maybe I'm being silly or something, but I would feel better if we didn't get too far away. And didn't you say that if he was coming back, this is the way he would come?" asked the hopeful redhead.

Tate smiled at the woman, nodded his head and said, "Yup, I did say that." He turned to gather up their gear and rig the horses for the day's travel. He was mindlessly whistling some happy tune while he saddled the horses and Maggie stood back, smiling at him.

"Now, that's better! Now you're acting happy instead of morose."

Tate turned to look at her and asked, "Mo what?"

"Morose, it means sullen or sad or deep in thought, that's all. Earlier you had a real serious expression but now you sound happy. I like that."

"Oh, you do, do you? Well, how 'bout helpin' with that gear so we can get on our happy way?"

CHAPTER TWENTY-SIX
TRACKERS

THE BIG IRISHMAN LET THE DAPPLE-GREY HAVE HIS HEAD AS they worked their way down the side slope to the valley floor. He knew he would be exposed in the wide-open flats, but it was the easiest way to get to the tree-line and find a game trail to return to the spot of his diggings. It would still be two or three days before he would reach the valley of the Platte that held both the site for his cabin and the place of his diggings. He let his mind drift to thoughts of gold and the reunion with his family. He was struggling with the desire to get a lot of gold and have the riches he thought he wanted and needed, but knowing that would mean a return to the civilized life, with the crowded cities and all that women seemed to want. But since his time in the mountains, he only wanted to have a simple life here in the wilderness. Yet he also wanted his family with him, but could they be happy here in the mountains? He knew this was a dilemma that he would have to find an answer for, and soon. Perhaps he could get enough gold, return to the city and his family, and then convince them to come back to the mountains with him.

Maccabee did a stutter step, raised his head with ears forward and stopped. The big dapple-grey was focused on movement a considerable distance away in the bottom of the valley. Daniel looked, shaded his eyes as he stood in his stirrups, and saw four horsemen moving toward a broad low hill with scattered timber. His first glance at the hill and the pattern of timber on top made him think of a hard-shelled turtle struggling toward the mountains. He focused on the riders, then lifted his eyes in the direction they were moving. Between the hill and the timbered skirt of the mountain range was a beehive of activity that looked like ants from this distance, but he recognized the making of an Indian village.

Daniel knew he was in the open with the only semblance of cover being the thick buck brush that clung to the hillside. But straight before him was a horseshoe shaped mound and he could see water just beyond. He kneed his horse forward, kicked him up to a canter and headed for the protective cover of the hollow. He rounded the uphill point, reined in next to the treeline and dropped to the ground. He scrambled to the crest of the hillock and dropped to his belly to scan the valley and the distant village to see if there was any indication he had been seen. There was none. The riders had continued on into the village and the rest of the band was busy erecting their lodges and readying the encampment. Daniel relaxed and watched, fascinated by the coordinated activity, with everyone working on their own lodges, but the entire band seeming to work together.

He slid back away from the crest and sat up to look over the hollow with the small lake. It would make a good long-term camp, even an excellent site for a cabin, but too far away from his gold diggings. Now the problem he had to resolve was how to get past the Indian village to make it on south to his claim. It was approaching mid-day and he decided to take some time for his animals to feed and to take a bit of grub himself. In the mountains, one of the first lessons learned is to eat when you have the opportunity and Daniel had made it a point to not miss any opportunity.

Daniel went to the crest of the horseshoe shaped hill to get a better understanding of the surrounding area, he needed a route of escape to get safely away from the Indians and back on the trail to his diggings. As he crested the mound, he bellied down and searched the trees and hills above the Indian encampment. From what he could tell, he would need to stay well into the trees and far above the camp to safely make it past. But even in daylight, especially with the camp new in the area, there would be plenty of Indians in the woods gathering firewood for their cookfires, and the youngsters that would be prone to explore their new surroundings.

He looked to the sky and the cloudless canopy offered no reprieve, as he thought about the night before and the phase of the moon. He remembered the moon was just starting to wax toward full and with a starlit night to help, he might be able to find a game trail through the pines. He looked at the black forest and mentally charted his course. It would be rough country, and impossible to cross without a game trail to follow. When the pine forests were this thick, there would be too much deadfall to make it through without creating enough noise to be heard across the park. But if he was lucky, he could find a trail that had been used by elk and deer alike and would traverse the timber covered slopes and provide a way through. It was the only chance he would have, and he would have to take it.

He returned to his horses, removed the saddle and packs and tethered them near the trees but within reach of the grass. Then Daniel went to a shady spot to stretch out and get some shut-eye until dark came and he could make his

getaway. It was going to be a long night and a dangerous one
at that.

———

"See thar Dingus! I tol' ya we'd find his tracks!" B.O. was
pointing to the hoofprints coming from the trees into the
clearing at the crest of the long slope. "Those cain't be more'n
a day old." B.O. had dropped to the ground to get a closer
look at the tracks and looked back at Dingus, "You're s'posed
to be the tracker an' now I'm havin' to do your job fer ya."
The big man stood, stepped into his stirrup and swung back
aboard his horse as he berated his partner. "I swear. If'n
brains were gunpowder you ain't got 'nuff to blow yer nose!
Come on, let's git a move on." He kicked his horse as he
leaned over to get another look at the tracks. As they
approached the edge of the clearing, he saw the remains of a
fire ring, "See thar! That's where he spent last night. Let's hol'
up right'chere and walk up yonder to check out the park.
Don't wanna go rushin' out thar in the open an' get our heads
shot off, now, do we?"

B.O. stepped off the horse, ground tied him, and started
walking to the crest of the bald ridge. He stood at the crest
and looked over the broad expanse of the Bayou Salado that
stretched as far as the eye could see to the south of their
lookout. B.O. stuck his thumbs in his belt and scanned the
valley, noting a large brown mass several miles away, that he
recognized as a large herd of buffalo. It didn't appear to be
on the move and the animals were grazing undisturbed as
B.O. turned slightly to his right to see the tracks of the two
horses of the big Irishman. As he visually followed them to
see the trail pointing across the long slope and toward the
distant mountains, he saw movement. The big man suddenly
dropped to his knees and leaned back toward a nearby tree.

Even with the floppy brim of the felt hat, he shaded his eyes as he looked in the distance.

B.O. turned to Dingus, "There, between this slope and that funny lookin' hill yonder, does that look like a Injun camp?" he asked his partner as he pointed.

Dingus, also on one knee and shading his eyes from the late afternoon sun, looked in the direction indicated, leaned forward and squinted, "Yeah, shore looks like one. A big 'un at that!"

"Yeah, but looky thar, them's the tracks o' that big mick! You don't s'pose he ran into them Injuns, do ya?" asked B.O.

"By Jehoshaphat, I dunno B.O., but them tracks shore do head thataway. So, what're we gonna do now?" asked an exasperated Dingus.

B.O. backed away from the crest and began surveying the surrounding mountains. Finally, he said, "I'm thinkin' we can backtrack a mite to the back side of this hyar hill," pointing to the timbered hill to the west, "and we can cut back acrost it and get behind that Injun camp. If that big Irish was smart, he'd stay in the timber and move on around 'em and if'n he did, then we can pick up his trail agin."

"Yeah, that sounds good B.O., you shore are smart, yessir."

With the long ridgeback hill between them and the Indian encampment, B.O. and Dingus were able to travel without concern of being seen. With daylight fading, they found a likely campsite in a grove of aspen and turned in for the night. B.O. was confident they would once again find the trail of Daniel O'Shaunessy that would eventually lead them to the source of the Irishman's gold. The big man was smiling at the thought of gold as he drifted off to sleep.

CHAPTER TWENTY-SEVEN
TIMBER

DANIEL AWOKE TO THE HIGH-PITCHED YIP YIP OF COYOTES
sending their love notes across the wide park. The cicadas
were scratching their nightly serenade on their out-of-tune
winged fiddles and the nighthawk circled overhead with his
eerie cry into the darkness. He judged the time to be nearing
midnight and he rose to rig his horses and get started.

The route he chose took him into a narrow ravine with a
small stream and well into the thicker timber. After a little
less than an hour, he pointed his gelding to the timbered
slope to the left of the stream where he would begin his
search for a game trail. He lifted his eyes to the night sky, saw
a star-studded canopy with the arching Milky Way
stretching to greet the moon that showed the first quarter
and hung lazily in the east behind him. After crossing the
stream and searching the bank for a break in the brush that
would invite the nocturnal drinkers, he found a bared trail
that cut the grassy bank. His eyes turned to the tree-line, saw
the break in the pines and pointed his horse to the dark maw
of the forest.

With a patchwork of moonlight and shadows, Maccabee

found the trail and stepped out with his rambling gait. Daniel had come to trust the sure-footed smart mountain horse and let him have his head. The pack-horse didn't hesitate to follow, confident in the leading of Maccabee and Daniel. The hard-packed trail was well-covered with pine needles and they moved quietly through the spruce and fir and occasional ponderosa pine. When they came to a broad dip between ridges that was thick with aspen, Daniel slowed the pace of the horses, allowing Maccabee to carefully pick his footing on the slick leaf-covered path.

After about three hours, Daniel estimated they were at least even with the camp or maybe slightly past it, but clouds were moving to hide the stars and moon and the trail was dark, slowing their progress. Although the vision of the horses had become accustomed to the darkness, they still had to be cautious in the deeper shadows as the tall spruce together with the dark clouds made the black of night almost impenetrable. They had passed through a wider valley that Daniel had mentally marked as the one with the stream that led to the encampment, and now were on the downhill side of a long ridge beyond. He was beginning to breathe a little easier, thinking they were past the Indian village.

Suddenly, a bolt of lightning parted the darkness before them with such suddenness and brightness to startle both Daniel and the animals. Although each one jumped a bit, Daniel held a taut rein and kept control. Maccabee lowered his head and continued his hopping slide down the steep slope. Once in the bottom, the lightning flashed again, an explosion of thunder followed and echoed across the narrow valley. Rain fell as if thrown from a bucket and immediately drenched Daniel and his animals. He searched for any place of refuge, and in the next lightning strike, saw a rock overhang at the edge of a talus slope that fell into the streambed. He pointed the animals to the rock wall, dropped to the ground and drew the horses closer. It wasn't enough to give complete shelter, but just enough, if they stood close to the wall, to keep the worst of the downpour away. Daniel stood, stroking the face of Maccabee, and talking to both the animals to reassure them and himself as well.

With no let-up to the storm, Daniel loosened the cinches for the horses, and with his bedroll blankets in hand, he sat down, back against the wall, and prepared to wait it out. The drenching continued for another couple of hours before finally letting up as the thin line of gray marked the eastern horizon. Daniel stood, shook out his blankets, tightened the cinches and mounted up to put a little more distance between him and the village.

The trail was muddy in spots, but the side slope had good run-off and the thick carpet of pine needles shed the water easily. Maccabee was confident of his footing and kept his rambling gait along the slope of the timbered skirts of the tall granite peaked mountains. As the sun bent its rays through the pines, Daniel's spirit lifted, and he breathed deep of the fresh washed mountain air. He smiled to himself, reached down and patted Maccabee's neck, "Good boy, good boy. You're the best horse a man could have, aye, that you are." He sat upright and searched the woods around and whenever a gap showed the valley below, he filled his eyes with the beauty of the sunlit plains.

After rounding a long finger of foothills that pointed out into the park, Daniel came to a wide valley with a good stream in the bottom and good cover nearby. He reined his horses to the glade, stepped down and started making camp. He didn't want to stay the entire day, but both he and the horses needed rest and he pined for some hot coffee. Also, the stream seemed to beckon the man with his gold pan.

———

B.O. AND DINGUS had hunkered down under their oilskin covers when the deluge hit in the night. Their camp was on a good slope and they had little to worry about, but the continuous downfall made sleeping difficult. After the worst of it let up, they dropped off into a fitful sleep, but the morning light roused the two from their blankets. As Dingus flipped the oilskin back, he looked to B.O., still unmoving, and hollered, "Whooooeeee! That was some storm!" Seeing no movement from his partner, Dingus begrudgingly got up and dug through their gear for the coffee pot. He brought it to the wet fire ring, sat it down, and went in search of some reasonably dry wood. When he returned with an armful of dead branches broken from the trunk of a big ponderosa with outspread branches that kept these dry, he was pleased with himself and dropped the branches in the fire pit to start their morning coffee. After several tries with flint and steel, the tinder showed a tiny glow and he dropped to all fours to blow and feed the beginning of their fire.

B.O. didn't stir until he smelled the coffee and when he approached the fire, he was grumpy and contentious as he growled, "Gimme a cup o' that!"

"Sure, B.O." replied Dingus, pouring his partner a cup of steaming black brew, "Here ya go." Dingus knew better than say much to the quarrelsome B.O. until the man was full awake and had at least two cups of java. Dingus sat back on the nearby log, cradling his own cup of coffee between his cold hands. As he brought it to his lips, he looked across at B.O. sitting with eyes closed and holding the cup at his chin. Dingus dared to speak, "That storm's gonna make it hard to find that feller's tracks, don'tcha think, B.O.?"

B.O. grunted, but said nothing, choosing to sip his coffee instead. Dingus shut up and waited for the irritable man to make the next move. Slowly B.O. opened his eyes, started a coughing fit and spilled his coffee as he fought the hacking, then he stood, ordering, "Pour me 'nother cup!" as he pointed to the cup in the dirt. Dingus jumped for the cup, wiped it out and filled it with coffee and cautiously handed it to B.O. who had once again seated himself.

B.O. took a deep gulp of coffee, and looked to Dingus, "We'll do whut we done afore. We'll head out like we was gonna do, an' check the cricks an' such, till we find his tracks. It worked before, should work agin'!"

"Sure B.O., whatever you say, B.O. An' like you said, we don' wanna git too close to him nohow," answered Dingus, attempting to pacify his friend. He had suffered one too many backhands from the big man to risk any more. The last time he hit the ground so hard it knocked him out and he had a headache for two days. It was best to walk softly around the big man whenever he had his hackles up.

It was mid-afternoon when they crested the ridge to once again look over the wide park below. Stopping at a slight clearing, the men looked to the valley floor toward the Indian encampment. With about forty lodges, it was a size-able camp and would have too many warriors to risk any confrontation. B.O. searched the hillsides for a possible route to circumvent the camp and decided on a way that would take them well above the valley floor and into the black timber. It would be difficult going, but it would also be safer. Pointing to the hillsides he said to Dingus, "We'll head off yonder to that valley thar, an' then we'll cut 'crost them hills to go round behind that camp. Should find a game trail through them woods thar, don'tcha think?"

"Sounds reasonable, B.O., you wanna lead out or ya' want me to?"

"You just foller 'long an' keep yore eyes open. No sleepin' in the saddle like ya usually do," ordered B.O. as he kneed his horse down the tree covered slope.

CHAPTER TWENTY-EIGHT
WOLVES

THE DISTANT HOWL OF A WOLF MADE THE SLEEPING TATE AND Maggie stir a little, but Lobo came instantly and fully awake, his head up and swiveling, searching for the source of the midnight call. The howl lifted again, and Lobo was on all fours, head up and pointing in the direction of the call. He trotted to the edge of the clearing, paused, and listened. Again, the howl sounded and Lobo lifted his head and answered with an eerie *ooowwooooooOOooooOOOoooo*, that trailed off into the darkness but was answered by the distant wail. Lobo turned to look at Tate, now sitting up and watching the wolf, saw the man lift his hand and nod his head, then the big beast trotted off into the black timber. Maggie looked at Tate and asked, "What is it? What's wrong?"

Tate turned to look at the woman, smiled, "Oh, probably nothing. Lobo was just talkin' to some of his kinfolks and decided to go see 'em I guess."

Maggie twisted around, looking for the wolf and back at Tate, "Will he be back?"

"Probably, I hope so anyway. Might just be love in the air, I dunno." Tate was staring at the break in the trees where

Lobo disappeared. He didn't see the smile that crossed the face of Maggie and she dropped back into her blankets to stare across the coals at Tate.

"I guess we'll just have to try to get a little more sleep an' hope he's back 'fore we leave." He fell back into his blankets, back to the fire and facing the trees as if he could see the wolf loping across the clearing in search of the distant caller. He knew it was a natural thing for the breed to find its like kind and mate. He had wondered about Lobo from the time he first took him in and nursed him as a pup, always knowing the day would come when he would search for a mate, but like most parents, he tried to put it off as long as possible. Now he thought about his friend and hoped he would return. It just wouldn't be the same without him.

When first light came, Tate was saddling the horses and had the coffee brewing, but Lobo was nowhere to be found. Tate's disappointment and concern were evident as he continually searched the edges of the clearing hoping to see the wolf return. Maggie didn't say anything, choosing to leave the man to his thoughts, as she helped with the last of the packing and clearing of their camp. With one last look around, Tate said, "Well, I guess we need to go. Ya' ready?"

"If you are, I am," answered Maggie, also looking around. She had grown to love the wolf as well and wished for his return but knew she was powerless to do anything. She looked to the gloomy man and said, "He'll be back, I'm sure of it. You'll see."

Tate forced a smile and answered, "Sure." He mounted up and reached for the lead rope of the packhorse, looked to see if Maggie was ready, and started to the trail. Their plan for the day was to ride the lower edge of the trees, and whenever they came to a stream, they would follow it up for a half mile or so, checking for diggings or other sign, and then continue their trek. It was a quiet start to the journey, with both allowing their thoughts to linger on the missing wolf.

The finger foothills that extended from the tall mountains usually had timber on the north side and grass and sage on the bald south side. Their route was a winding up and down one that followed an assortment of game trails that led from the mountains to the park and water below. It was early afternoon when they came to a slight valley at the head of a long red soil ridge that stretched into the park but paralleled the mountains. Sitting apart from the other mountains, separated by a saddle crossing, was a bald mountain that stood as a sentinel over the valley beyond and the park below. They stopped for a midday break and the beginning of their brief exploration of the stream bed in the little valley.

"Boy oh boy, there musta been one big thunderstorm come through here last night. Look how wet everything is, and that creek there's muddy still. I heard some thunder, but thought it was farther east. Did you hear it?" asked Tate as he stepped down from the saddle.

"Yes, but it sounded too far away, and I was so tired, I went right back to sleep." Maggie looked at Tate as he stood with his hands lifted to help her from her horse. "My, aren't you the gentleman," she smiled as she leaned toward him to accept his offered assistance. "To what do I owe this honor, Mr. Saint?" she teased as she smiled at him.

"Oh, uh, well, it's so muddy around here an all, I just thought I'd help ya' to the grass so ya' wouldn't get all muddy's all." He ducked his head, embarrassed.

"Well, I'm mighty thankful sir. That's very kind of you and I appreciate it." She lifted her eyes to the views around her, saw movement in the grass beyond the stream and leaned to see better. She turned to Tate and said, "Look! Isn't that Lobo?"

In the tall grass there were two wolves running and

cavorting as if there were no other creatures anywhere around. The larger one, undoubtedly Lobo, chased after the darker and smaller one. As soon as he came near, the smaller wolf would drop to the ground, roll to her back and playfully paw at Lobo. Then she would jump up and trot off, looking back to see if he would follow.

Tate was watching and let a slow grin cross his face, "Looks like he found himself a girlfriend."

"Will he come back?" asked Maggie, watching the two romp in the grass.

"Oh, he knows we're here. That's probably why he's playin' around out there, just to show us he's near. He'll probably be back, might even bring her with him, hard tellin' though."

"Well, he looks like he's having fun anyway. But I hope he comes back."

After their noon stop, they followed the creek upstream as they planned, but found no sign of anyone prospecting and few beaver ponds. They turned back downstream and followed a trail that stayed just in the tree-line and circled the bald topped mountain on the park side. It was late afternoon when they faced the wide valley on the north side of the bald mountain and Tate pointed Shady up stream into the draw, searching for the camp for the night. Their foray upstream showed lots of sign of beaver but again there were no prospect holes. Tate spotted a campsite in a grove of aspen and motioned to Maggie as they started for it. Then Tate looked at the edge of the stream and saw tracks. He reined up, leaned down, and looking back at Maggie, motioned for her to stop as he stepped down for a closer look.

He knelt beside the tracks, looked closely and followed the outline with his fingertips, reading the sign carefully. He lifted his eyes to follow the tracks as they led off toward the saddle cut between the bald mountain and the larger granite tipped peaks. He looked back at the tracks and stood to turn toward Maggie.

"Somebody was here, probably last night, maybe this morning. Two horses, both loaded, carryin' heavy, and went off thataway. Don't think they were Indians."

"Oh Tate! Do you think . . .?"

"I dunno, but let's make camp up there in the trees. Then we can check aroun' for any other sign."

As they walked into the clearing, they both saw the remains of the fire and knew this was where the riders of the two horses had camped for the night. Tate walked around, looking at the tracks and other sign, occasionally kneeling to look closer, then he stood, looking to Maggie, "I think it was just one man. A big man, but he was wearing moccasins. So, no tellin' who he might be, could just be a trapper lookin' for beaver or maybe a buffalo hunter scoutin' buffalo. Don't know. But, let's make camp and then we'll check down by the stream for any prospectin' sign."

Maggie nodded her head and hurried to help de-rig the packhorse and unsaddle her horse. She was anxious for any sign that might confirm the mysterious traveler was her father, but she was also cautious and sought to temper her excitement, knowing Tate was right and it could be anyone. But she hurried in her tasks, nevertheless and hopeful still.

CHAPTER TWENTY-NINE
TRACKS

LOBO WAS BACK. THE FIRST THING TATE SAW WHEN HE OPENED his eyes before first light, was the ruffled fur of the big wolf as he stretched out beside his friend. Tate reached over and ran his hands through the scruff of the wolf's neck and whispered, "Welcome back, boy." He lifted one eyelid to peer at his friend, dropped it shut and remained unmoving. Tate stretched his arms over his head, pushed back his blankets and sat up to look around the quiet camp. Maggie's blankets were rumpled and empty and Tate searched the trees in the darkness for any movement other than the three horses standing hipshot and flipping their ears and occasionally their tails. He stood, causing Lobo to stand as well, and walked to the edge of the clearing to see the stretch of grass between their camp and the creek. Standing alone, arms folded across her chest, was the redhead staring in the moonlight at the tracks from the day before.

Tate walked up behind her and said, "I know you hope it's your father, but we have no way of knowing for certain." She was startled and whirled around to face him, she dropped her arms and walked to him, leaning her head on his chest.

He naturally put his arms around her to comfort her as she said, "I know, but I, uh, we have been looking for so long, I so want it to be him."

She lifted her face to his and he answered, "I know. And I hope it is him, but I was also thinkin' that if it's not him and we take off chasin' after the maker of these tracks, we might get ourselves into trouble or at the least, we'd miss a chance of finding out more about your father or even running into the real Daniel O'Shaunessy."

"What do you mean?" asked the redhead.

"Well, we're already here. I think we need to do like we've been doin' and move on upstream, look for any other diggings or other sign, and if we don't find any, then we decide to go farther north or turn back to see if that was your father. If it is, then we'll find him at those diggings on the Platte, but if it's not, whoever made those tracks will go on about his merry way and we won't have wasted this trip into this valley for nothing."

She put her forehead back on his chest and playfully hit him with her balled up fist, saying, "Tate, sometimes you're just too practical. You're right, I know, so, let's have our coffee and leftovers and then we'll go upstream." She had leaned back in his arms to look up at his face, smiled at him as he let her go and they walked side by side back to the camp.

As the sun climbed over the eastern horizon, Tate and Maggie felt its warmth on their backs. Lobo was scouting the trail before them as they rode alongside the cascading stream coming from the high mountains. When the sun was well up they came to a string of beaver ponds, nestled in the creek bottom and surrounded by aspen. The beavers had been busy as dam after dam held back the mountain run off. The slap of beaver tails on the water told the fur family to head to their haven of a branch covered hut amid the pond. Several gnawed stumps showed grey telling Tate the beavers had been here for several seasons, and freshly felled trees told of many current inhabitants.

They reined up beside one of the ponds and Tate stepped down to have a better look. He walked along the side of the pond, looking for any indication that traps had been set, but seeing none, he mounted up and said, "Let's go a bit further, then we'll be certain." Maggie nodded and kneed her pinto to follow Tate and the packhorse. They continually scanned the creek bank for any sign of digging or panning or the use of a rocker. Most prospectors pay little attention to the signs they leave behind of their digging and more, for their attention is only on the next pan or shovel full and the possibility of gold. What they leave behind is of no concern to them.

When they came to another string of beaver ponds that proved unproductive, Tate said, "Alright, I think we've come far enough. It appears no one has been prospecting or trapping up this stream, at least not as far as we can tell and certainly not recently. So, let's head on back, and I'm thinkin' maybe we should follow that feller's tracks and see where he goes."

Maggie let a big smile cross her face as she turned the pinto around and over her shoulder said, "I was hoping you'd say that."

Tate chuckled at the girl as he replied, "I know you were, but I just wanted to be sure. He could've come up here and found a richer pocket and never return to the one down yonder. Then we'd miss him altogether."

———

"SEE THERE, tol'ja. Them's his tracks, sure 'nuff," snarled B.O. He sat on his horse, looking down at Dingus as the man examined the tracks that led away from the rock overhang and started through the timber.

"Yup, looks like they was made yes'tiddy mornin', after that rain quit," observed Dingus. "An' with all this wet ground, he'll be easy follerin' now."

"Wal, come'on and let's get a move on," ordered B.O., impatient with his tracker.

It was just after first light when they found the tracks, having camped in the same draw the night before. With renewed determination, they were certain they would find their quarry before the day was out and hopefully he would be where ever he had found the gold he used at the traders. Dingus led the way, trailing their packhorse with their dwindling supplies, followed by the boisterous B.O. who continually derided his partner if for no other reason than to exert his assumed authority over the man.

They broke from the trees where the creek made a wide bend and traveled over the broad crossing. They moved through the water, but once on the opposite side, Dingus stopped, looking down at the tracks they had been following. He stepped down as B.O. bumped his horse coming from the stream. Down on one knee, Dingus stretched his hand down to more closely examine the tracks. He stood, looking around, then turned to B.O., "There's other tracks here. Near as I can make out, three horses crossed, coming from down yonder," pointing downstream to the mouth of the valley, "and moving upstream there. Two people, both wearin' moccasins, an' I think one of 'ems a woman. Three horses, one a packhorse. Could be Injuns, mebbe a brave an' his squaw. They took a good look at these tracks we're a follerin' but they went on upstream."

B.O. stood in his stirrups to look above the willows at streamside, and seeing nothing, "Wal, I ain't concerned about a couple Injuns. Since they went up thar, it don't concern us. An' if'n they come back, we'll be long gone. Let's keep after the big mick."

"Alright, B.O., whatever you say," answered Dingus as he mounted up to follow the tracks of the Irishman.

CHAPTER THIRTY
CONVERGENCE

By midday, Tate and Maggie were almost back to the camp of the night before. They pushed on to get to the camp and have their midday break for the horses and themselves to get a bite of food. When he slipped from the saddle, he loosened the cinches for the horses, grabbed the coffee pot from the pack and went to the fire circle where Maggie sat waiting. Her glassy-eyed stare said she was deep in thought yet undoubtedly anxious to catch up with the man she was certain was her father. Single-minded, she was not concerned about coffee or food.

Tate built a small fire and started the coffee as he sat back and watched the somewhat sullen woman staring at the small flames. Tate left her to her reverie, more concerned about the horses than himself and Maggie, and poured himself a cup of coffee. He stood to take a stroll to stretch his legs and started towards the creek when Maggie said, "Wait for me!" She jumped and trotted after Tate, not wanting to be alone even for a short while. She put her hand in the crook of his arm and walked beside him quietly, still thinking.

"Are you still worryin' 'bout your Pa?" asked Tate.

"No, just thinking about everything. If that is my father, what will he want to do, and where he will want to go? I'm not sure my place is with him now, what with Mum gone," she mused.

"And if you didn't go with your father, where would you go?"

"Oh, I don't know, I should be out on my own. I've been on my own since Mum died and me father certainly doesn't need me, so . . ."

Tate chuckled, thinking *I've got a couple cabins, hmmm . . .* "Well, let's get ready to leave, we will have to cover a lot of country to get to his diggings before dark."

"You think we can?" asked Maggie, smiling excitedly.

"Maybe, dunno, but I guess we can try."

It was less than a hundred yards to the place where they first saw the tracks and as they approached, Tate's brow wrinkled when he saw something different. He reined up and dropped to the ground as Maggie pulled up beside Shady, looking at Tate as he knelt on one knee, examining the tracks. He stood and looked toward the saddle between the mountains, back across the creek and down at the tracks again. He looked up at Maggie, concern written on his face, "Somebody else has crossed here, and by the sign, they're followin' the first man." He pointed to the tracks, "See there, one of 'em knelt and looked real close at the tracks, he wore moccasins, but I don't think he was an Indian. The stitching on the side, and the wear on the bottom shows someone that doesn't take care of his foot gear. It looks like three horses, could be two or three riders or two and a packhorse, but they're definitely following the big fella."

"What does that mean?" asked Maggie, fearful of the answer.

"Oh, I dunno," drawled Tate, not wanting to scare the woman, but needing to be truthful with her, she deserved that. "It could be they're after somethin' he has, or they think he has. They could just be after his gear, you know, his horses, rifle, supplies and such. Then again, it could be just two fellas goin' the same way and lookin' to catch up with the big fella, might be a friend o' theirs. I wouldn't be worryin' 'bout it." He took one last look at the tracks, making special note of each one. Horses have a distinctive track, some are shod with metal horseshoes, and even those are distinctive with size and shape, and others, unshod, have a distinguishing size, shape and marks. Those unique tracks make it easy for a good tracker to determine which horse went what direction. Tate had become very skilled at tracking, learning first from Kit Carson, then the Comanche and others.

He mounted Shady, looked up the slope to the notch between the mountains with the saddle crossing that had been taken by both the big man and the two followers. Tate looked to Maggie, "Ya know, we've come across that country and we know where his diggings are, I'm thinkin' we can go higher on the mountain and come out in that valley of the Platte upstream of his diggings and probably beat 'em all. Or, at least beat the two that are followin'."

"Can we? Because if we can, maybe we can keep something bad from happening," pleaded Maggie, worried about the man she hoped was her father.

"It'll be hard goin', we'll be moving purty fast, and might hafta keep movin' after dark. But if you're up to it . . . "

"I'm game if you are!" declared the redhead as she kicked her pinto and started up the trail after the tracks. She looked over her shoulder at a surprised Tate, "Well, come on if you're comin'!"

Once they crested the saddle notch with the bald mountain standing between them and the wide park, Tate took the lead and pointed them across the timbered skirt of the peak that rose to touch the blue to the west of the trail. The thin timber made it easy to traverse the long slope that took them to the talus shoulder of the big mountain. Once atop that shoulder, they could see an easy game trail angling to the creek at the bottom of a long shallow draw. Another ridge, another draw, ever moving closer to timberline, and they broke from a large thicket of aspen onto a wide timbered knoll.

As fast as they were moving, usually at a trot, often at a canter, the sun was dropping faster. With Shady having a long-striding, ground eating gait, Tate often had to rein back for the smaller pinto ridden by Maggie. But the Indian pony showed its stamina as she pulled alongside the packhorse with its sides heaving from the long trek. Tate slowed their pace, but kept moving, wanting to reach the ridge above the river before dark. In just a short while, they crossed the wide knoll, came into a broad grassy park, and in the fading light, Tate could see down the slope to the distant park and knew they were close to the ridge above the river.

"Let's stop here, the horses are beat and there's a little spring-fed creek in the trees there and we could use some rest as well," directed Tate.

"You won't get any argument from me!" wheezed Maggie, as she practically rolled from her horse. She staggered to the creek and bellied down to drink deep of the cold clear water. Tate watched the redhead, chuckling at his remembrance of his first sight of the prim and proper woman and comparing that picture with this woman, on her belly, drinking straight from the little creek. Maggie pulled her knees under her and sat up, turning to look at Tate as she wiped the water from her face, chin and neck with her forearm. He smiled at her lack of inhibition, then knelt on one knee, dipped his hand in the water and brought it to his lips to enjoy the icy fresh snow melt.

When Tate sat back on his haunches to look at Maggie, he

began to explain, "That ridge," pointing with his chin, "is right above the river where your father's diggings are, but, we still don't know if the first set of tracks were made by him. If we go rushin' into that fella's camp, an' he's not your father, it might not be too healthy for us, and even if it is your Pa, he's not expectin' you and it could still be a mite dangerous. Most men of the mountains that last very long, do so by not being careless and lettin' anybody sneak up on 'em. So, here's what I'm thinkin'. We'll wait till after dark, the moon's gonna be purty bright tonight, an' we'll move down a bit closer. We'll be close enough, that if'n he gets into trouble, we can help him out. But, I'd rather not try goin' in to his camp in the dark."

"I understand," answered Maggie, somewhat dejected. "I know we can't push our horses anymore, they're lathered up now as it is," she looked at the horses taking a deep drink from the small stream below them. "Do you think we beat the other two here?"

"I believe so, but we won't know till we get closer. Right now, how 'bout you gettin' us some jerked venison and the rest o' that cornbread. We don't wanna fire, so, while you're doin' that, I'll tend to the horses."

The moon was already showing its bright half face when Tate finished saddling the horses. He nudged the sleeping Maggie with his toe and said, "Come'on sleepyhead, git a move on. We ain't gonna have light much longer, those clouds'll cover up that ol' man in the moon and it'll soon be too dark to move." The trail angled down through the trees, making an easy traverse of the pine covered hill that over-shadowed the river. Once off the slope, the wide bank of the Platte glistened with the dew-covered grass and willows. The moonlight reflected off the ripples where they crossed, and the stillness of the night enveloped the easy moving travelers. Tate led them to the edge of the timber that came from the far-side slope, pushed into the trees to a small clearing that would suffice for their night's camp.

They quietly stripped the gear from the animals and stretched out the bedrolls. Tate stood beside Maggie as he quietly instructed, "Keep your rifle beside you, but go 'head on and try to get some sleep. Me'n Lobo's gonna try to sneak off through these trees and see where all them other fellas are campin'. They might not be anywhere around, but I wanna make sure." He looked around their camp, "This is a good site, can't be seen less you're right up close. If you get concerned about anything, just watch the horses, they'll be your watchdog for the night. If they get to stirrin' and lift their heads to look around, then quickly move back into those trees and take cover. I'm sure nothin's gonna happen, but better safe than sorry."

"I understand. I'll be fine. You just be careful and make sure you come back." She leaned against him, shoulder to shoulder, to emphasize her directions. He looked down at her, smiled, and said, "Ah, Lobo'll take care of me, you know that."

CHAPTER THIRTY-ONE
CONFRONTATION

THE BOTTOM OF THE VALLEY HELD THE MEANDERING RIVER marked by willows, cattail bogs, quicksand, and patches of grass. Apart from the river bottom, grass, rabbit brush, and scrub oak held to the flats that reached to the tree-line of aspen, juniper and pine. The trees provided the only logical place to camp, giving good cover within the towering pines. It was through these scattered pines and junipers that Tate followed Lobo as they searched for any sign of the big man and his pursuers.

Whenever the moon peeked out of the clouds, Tate could mark his location by the terrain and the hillside across the river and he knew they were nearing the site of the discovered diggings. Tate stopped, knelt down, and motioned for Lobo to come to his side. Slowly and methodically, Tate searched the grassy flat and through the trees, knowing he probably would not see the camp except for the presence of horses. He drew in a deep breath, searching for the smell of a campfire or horses. Lobo was the first to show recognition, as he took one step forward, moving slow, holding the other front foot cocked and still, his nostrils flaring. He turned to look at Tate, who had picked up the scent of lathered horses and manure. They were near. Tate dropped to all fours, bow in hand, looking between and beneath the trees, waiting. His breathing was deep but measured, knowing the horses could just as easily smell him and the wolf, and he moved slowly forward.

The snort of a horse sounded, and Tate and Lobo dropped to their bellies, unmoving, waiting. Another horse stomped and swished his tail, probably at a buck-fly, and another snort then they were still. No other sound gave evidence of alarm and Tate motioned for Lobo to stay. With his bow now across his back, Tate moved on his belly, slowly, imperceptibly, quietly. Close to twenty yards from the camp, he smelled smoke from an earlier fire, heard the occasional movements of the horses, and the snorting and snoring of a sleeping man. Only two horses stood at the picket line, one bedroll with a big man showed near the tree-line and packs and gear made a stack nearby. Satisfied this was the big man's camp, Tate began his retreat, moving just as slowly as before.

Lobo stood to all fours to welcome his master back but made no noise. Tate rubbed the scruff of the wolf's neck and motioned for him to come with him. They circled wide and high to search for the camp of the followers. The pair ghosted through the woods with a pine needle carpet to still the sounds and when they broke from the aspen that marked the end of the wooded ridge, dropped toward the valley floor. No other camp had been sighted which could only mean one of two things: either the men had passed on by or were camped on the opposite side of the river. Tate decided to return to his camp by way of following the willows at the river bank. There were some clusters of cottonwood and alders as well as thick chokecherry brush that offered cover and concealment for their return jaunt. As they approached their camp, the dim band of grey was marking the eastern horizon.

Maggie's blankets were rumpled but empty. Standing with his silhouette masked by the black timber, Tate imitated the thweet thweet of the nighthawk, a signal previously agreed upon between the two. Across the small clearing, a shadow moved and silently stepped into the open, revealing the figure of Maggie, rifle at the ready. Tate chuckled and stepped from the timber and spoke softly, "You're gettin' plum sneaky, but smart."

"Had a good teacher," she answered as the starlight shone through her red hair and the moon cleared the clouds long enough to show her smile. "Did you find him?"

"Well, I found the camp of a big man traveling alone, but I couldn't tell if it was your father or not. Didn't find the camp of the others, though."

"So, what do we do now?" asked Maggie.

"Well, I figger, 'bout first light, we go down to the big feller's camp and get your question answered."

"My question?" she queried, forehead wrinkling in wonder.

"If'n that man's your father."

She smiled and sat down heavily on a big flat rock beside them. She looked at the sky, trying to will it to become daylight, and back at Tate with a broad grin on her face. "Maybe our search is over, I hope so anyway."

Tate sat down beside her, Lobo went to her feet and lay his head in her lap and she thought how these were her two favorite creatures. She smiled at the thought and Tate asked, "O.K., what is it?"

"Oh, nothing. Just anxious is all."

Tate saddled the horses by the dim light of early grey and turned to Maggie, who stood well behind him, anxiously pacing back and forth, and then he looked at Lobo, "Boy, if'n I'da let her and just pointed her in the right direction, she'd already be there by now at that pace." Maggie looked at him and walked briskly toward him, veered aside and went to her pinto and stepped aboard.

"Alright, you lead the way," she instructed.

"Now, wait just a minute, see, here's what I think we need to do . . . "

THE GREY SKY was slowly yielding to the threatening sun and the low-lying clouds had their bellies painted orange when Tate called out, "Hellooo the camp!"

He heard movement, then an answer, "Come on if you're friendly. Prepare to meet your maker if you're not."

Tate led the way walking and leading Shady with Lobo alongside. Behind him was the packhorse and leading her pinto, followed Maggie, who could not be clearly seen because of the horses. They walked slowly into the man's camp, but he was hidden. Then a voice came from the trees and said, "Lift your hands above your head an' keep comin'." The big man stepped from behind an even bigger tree and showed himself standing sideways, rifle cradled in his arm and pointed directly at Tate. He leaned to one side, saw the horses and someone behind them, "You too, behind the horses, raise your hands!"

Tate recognized the man from Maggie's description. A big man, five or six inches over six feet, easily close to three hundred pounds, big bushy red beard and a bush of red hair stuffed under a plaid Tam O'Shanter. Tate smiled and asked, "And would your name be Daniel Patrick O'Shaunessy?"

The man cocked his head to the side, faced full forward and with his brow wrinkling, "Aye, an' how be ye knowin' me name?"

Maggie could stay behind no longer for she had recognized her father's voice. He had no sooner asked the question than she came running from behind Tate and rushed toward her father. He barely had time to see her, much less recognize her, when she stopped directly in front of the big man, grinning up at his confounded face and said, "Don't ye even know your own daughter?"

Daniel stuttered, looking down at the girl, "Ma . . .Mar . . . Margarite? Is it you?"

She jumped into his arms, threw her arms around his neck and buried her face in his beard and started sobbing. Neither would let loose of the other as Daniel danced around in a circle, holding his daughter with her feet off the ground, "Praise be the Lord, Praise be Jesus!"

Tate led the horses to the side, dropped their reins to ground tie them, and turned to watch the reunion. Lobo stood at his side, watching the curious sight of the two Irish.

A snap of a stick from back in the trees caught Tate's attention at the same time Lobo tensed and let a low growl come forth. Tate spun around to see the toothless grin of a man with grey whiskers, dirty grey homespun shirt, buckskin britches, and holding a rifle pointed at Tate's belly. Lobo turned, and Tate looked to see what moved the wolf. Sitting on a horse was a big man with eyes too close, and bushy mutton-chop whiskers, holding a rifle across his pommel, pointed at Daniel and Maggie. The buck brush at the edge of the clearing had obscured the intruder's vision of Lobo and the wolf had slipped from the clearing, unnoticed.

"Wal, now, ain't that a purty sight!" cackled B.O. as he looked at Daniel and Maggie, standing arm in arm. Daniel slowly stepped in front of Maggie, pushing her behind him. Tate noticed the move, and stepped forward, allowing his arm to drop to his side to hide the Paterson. Daniel spoke up,

"What is it you want? I haven't even started the coffee yet, ran out some time ago."

B.O. laughed, causing Dingus to laugh as well, and B.O. said, "Oh, we don't want your coffee, do we Dingus?"

"Hehehee, no, we don't want your coffee. But you know B.O., that redhead might be nice!" answered Dingus from the trees. He started pushing his way through the brush and Tate saw his chance. He brought the Paterson up and shot B.O., causing him to squeeze the trigger on his rifle with a roar and a cloud of grey smoke emitting from the muzzle. At the same time a streak of grey hit Dingus, bearing him to the ground. Tate looked at B.O., red had blossomed on his chest, but he still sat his horse. He growled as he looked at Tate, kicked his horse in a charging lunge toward the man, and saw smoke and fire come from the pistol again. Tate fired, cocked the hammer, fired again, and again, and again. The big man's chest and belly showed red and with each shot, dust and dirt puffed from his dirty clothes, but still he came, kicking his horse in a frenzy. Tate dove to the side, just behind a small stack of firewood that the horse hit with his hooves as he leaped over the fallen man. The jump of the horse caused B.O. to lose his grip and his seat and he fell over backwards, bouncing off the rump of the horse as the animal swerved to miss a tree. The bone-crunching thud of the fat man hitting the ground told of broken bones, but the man felt nothing. He was dead before he hit the ground.

The growl and snarl and snapping of teeth of the wolf came from behind the thick buck brush. The screams of Dingus were quickly muffled when his throat was clamped between the powerful jaws of the wolf. Unseen by the others, Lobo shook his head side to side as he tore the throat from the man and the limp body hung loosely between his front legs.

"Lobo!" shouted Tate, and Lobo let loose his prey, and

bounded into the clearing to his friend. Blood covered the wolf's chest, forelegs, and jowls, but the wolf still seemed to smile at Tate as he came to him. Tate ran his fingers through the scruff of Lobo's neck and lifted his eyes to see Maggie kneeling beside the prone figure of her father, sobbing.

CHAPTER THIRTY-TWO
CARE

TATE RAN TO THE SIDE OF MAGGIE, DROPPED TO HIS KNEES TO examine Daniel's wound. The big man moaned, and his eyes fluttered open to see the concerned face of Maggie, eyes tearing up as Tate said, "He's hit purty hard, but . . . "

The wide-eyed Daniel interrupted, "It canna be too bad, I'm still kicking." He put his big meaty hand over Maggie's that rested on his chest, "I will be fine, lassie, you'll see. Takes more'n that to down an Irishman!"

Tate urged the big man to roll to his side so he could check his back. "It went through," and looking at Maggie, "Get some cloth outta the packs, tear up whatever you find and pack these wounds. I'll make a poultice."

Each hurried to their task and as Maggie applied folded cloth to the wounds, Tate was making a poultice from cattail and sage leaves. Within moments, the mashed combination was formed into pancakes of greenish brown mush that Tate packed on the entry and exit of the bullet wound. Once the poultice was applied, he covered them with thick pads of cloth and with long strips of buckskin cut from the britches of the intruders, Daniel was soon bandaged and bound. Tate let the big man lie back down, and as he stood, he said, "I'm gonna make a travois. We'll take him to the Ute camp and get some help tendin' to him. I'm sure White Buffalo Horn and Singing Bird know a few things that'll help him heal up."

Maggie looked up at Tate, "Are you sure? Will it be alright to move him? He lost a lot of blood." Worry painted her face as she looked from Tate to the pale figure of her father.

"That kinda wound, low down on the shoulder like that, needs a lot o' care. We can't risk it gettin' infected and he's gonna need all the care he can get," surmised Tate. He looked at Maggie, concern showing in his eyes, "Look, I know you're scared and rightly so, but I don't know much more to do to help him and I've seen some Shaman's use things I never heard of to help folks get better. That's the closest thing we're gonna get to a doctor an' I'm sure Singing Bird would want to help too, so, yeah, let's be for doin' this."

Maggie searched his eyes and seeing his concern, she looked at her father who forced a smile and a nod, and she said, "Alright, we'll do it."

Tate went to the trees in search of some long slender saplings, knowing he would have to use aspen rather than the preferred lodgepole pine that didn't grow at this elevation. He also found the tied horse that apparently belonged to one of the intruders and he unsaddled him and set him loose with a slap on the rump. After checking the saddle bags for anything of use, he returned to the task of the poles.

The big horse of B.O. had gone to the side of the picketed horses of Tate and company and was now chosen to bear the travois. Tate used the gear to fashion the travois and hang it from the withers of the animal. With the blankets from the intruders, a comfortable transport was soon completed and with the help of both Maggie and Tate, Daniel was soon lying on the wilderness stretcher.

With Tate leading the string of Daniel's horse and packhorse and their own, and Maggie leading the big bay and the travois, they started to the village. With one stop for a short rest for both animals and travelers, it was nearing dusk when the black forested hill that marked the mouth of the valley of the village showed itself. By the time they rode through the cut between the black hill and the bigger round top mountain, the dim light of dusk had chased the sun belowthe horizon.

When the outrider scouts sighted the visitors, they rode out yipping and shouting war cries as they waved their lances and coup sticks. Quickly recognizing the visitors, the taunting warriors became greeters of welcome and accompanied the entourage into the village. Singing Bird ran up to them, saw the travois, and looked at Maggie for an answer. "It's me father, he's been shot and needs some care. Do you think your grandfather will allow us the use of a lodge?"

"Yes, yes," then looking to Tate, "You go to Lame Buffalo, I will take Morning Sky and her father to the lodge." No longer the timid girl they rescued in the mountains, Singing Bird was now a confident leader of her people. She stopped them in front of a lodge, went to the entry flap, scratched, and when Little Otter stepped out, Singing Bird quickly explained. The three women started to help the now unconscious Daniel from the travois but had to summon help from four men. They derigged the travois and used it as a stretcher to carry the man into the tipi.

Tate made his obligatory greetings to Lame Buffalo and was warmly welcomed by the chief of the Yamparika Ute band. As he led his horses to the lodge of Little Otter, Lobo was approached by a boy that had made friends with him during their first visit. The boy dropped to his knees in front of the wolf to hug his neck and run his hands through his fur. The boy looked up to Tate, said something in Ute that Tate didn't understand but thought he caught the boy's intent and nodded his head in approval. The boy started off, pleading with Lobo to follow and the wolf, with a quick look to Tate for permission, trotted off with the boy.

"So, there you are! I thought we had lost you!" declared Maggie as Tate neared the lodge. "Father's still out of it, but Little Otter and Singing Bird are tending to him. They both said he will be fine and I'm very relieved. You were right, it's good that we came here."

Tate smiled at her as he began removing the gear from the horses, making quite a pile of saddles, packs, and more, beside the lodge. "Well, you might wanna prepare yourself. There might be some things they do you won't agree with, but just trust 'em. What they do they've been doin' for many years and some'o' their herbs and stuff are right fine medicines."

"I know, and you're right. He's a strong man, but it's hard for me to see him down like that. I never thought anything could put me father down, he just seemed invincible, but I know those are the thoughts of a child as I remembered him, a giant of a man."

"He's a big 'un alright," commented Tate, smiling.

Maggie returned the smile, releasing some of her tension and fear as she did. She looked at Tate as he started off with the horses, taking them to the village herd, and thought how he always made her feel secure, safe, even happy. Even at times like this when she was worried about her father, just the nearness of Tate gave her comfort and confidence that everything was going to be alright.

As Maggie stepped into the lodge, she saw Little Otter finishing the re-bandaging of the wounds. Daniel stirred and slowly opened his eyes, saw Little Otter smiling at him, looked at the hide lodge overhead, and turned his head to look around. Seeing Maggie, "Ah, lassie, I was beginnin' to think I'd died an' gone to glory, but you really are here." He

was forcing his words, speaking softer than his usual boisterous volume, "Where is here?"

"You are in the lodge of Little Otter," nodding her head
toward the woman, "she is our friend and we are in the
village of the Ute people. They are wonderful people and will
help you get better," declared Maggie. "Providing, of course,
that you do what you're told," she added sternly.

"Right now, I dinna think I am strong enough to do
otherwise," answered the red bearded man, breathing heavily
as he struggled to get comfortable. He had one hand behind
his head and the other to his side as he fought with the
blankets.

Little Otter pushed his hand aside, pulled the blankets up
around him, placed a folded blanket under his head then sat
back on her heels as she watched the interplay between
father and daughter. She smiled, stood, and started to the
entry. She quietly said to Maggie, "I will prepare a broth for
him. He needs to get his strength back and it will take
some time."

Daniel motioned for Maggie to come near and sit beside
him. "So, tell me everything, how's your mum?"

Maggie dropped her head and said, "Mum's gone, Da.
She died close to a year ago. That's why I came looking
for you."

The big man lay quiet and still for several moments and
he reached out to touch the hand of Maggie to share their
bond. For the next hour they shared memories, thoughts and
news of friends and events. As they grew more relaxed with
one another and became re-acquainted, Daniel asked, "And
just who is this man you're with?"

Maggie dropped her eyes, embarrassed, as she said, "He's
a friend that Kit Carson asked to help me find you. His name
is Tate Saint."

"And how long have you two been lookin' for me?"

"Seems like forever, but it's only been a couple months," she answered.

"And it has been just the two of ye together, all alone in these mountains, with no chaperone?" he asked sternly and wide-eyed.

"Oh, so now it's the concerned father that be askin' his daughter that he left behind 'bout how she's been behavin'?" exclaimed Maggie, standing to her feet and hands on her hips as her cheeks colored with indignation.

Daniel exploded in laughter, tried to sit up, grabbed his wound and scowled, and finally lay back. His broad smile showed through the red bushy beard as he said, "So, you're in love with him too?"

Maggie struggled to respond, "Uh . . .uh, oh you!" and sat back down at the side of her father. She dropped her head in her hands, shaking it side to side, and looked up at the grinning man, "I dunno. Maybe. I just don't know what I feel. I wish Mum were here so I could talk to her," she said, tears filling her green eyes. "I can't imagine myself without him, and I think he feels the same way, but . . . "

"Lassie, if I can see it, he can too. An' if it be the will of the Lord, then let it be," declared the big Irishman. "Just so long as he understands that if he dares to mistreat me daughter, he'll have me to answer to!"

Maggie lay her head on her father's massive chest and relished the moment together. This was what she had longed for and prayed for and she was determined this would not be the last time they were together.

The entry flap was pushed aside as Little Otter entered, carrying a carved bowl full of steaming broth for her patient. Maggie stood and moved aside and busied herself with preparing her bedroll and Tate's. Singing Bird now had a separate lodge, but they would share this lodge of Little Otter as they had done before.

CHAPTER THIRTY-THREE
COURTING

"GOOD MORNING!" SAID MAGGIE AS SHE CLIMBED THE LAST OF the hill to Tate's side. She sat down beside him, shoulder to shoulder and said, "Beautiful day, isn't it? I love it when the sky is nothing but blue, no clouds, just the big arch of blue overhead. This is such beautiful country!" she had drawn her knees up and wrapped her arms around them, laying her cheek on one and smiling at Tate.

"Yup, sure is, and I have to agree with you about the clear blue sky." He leaned back on stiff arms behind him, soaking up the morning sun on his face. They were on the shoulder of the round top hill beside the camp and facing the rising sun as it cleared the eastern horizon and washed away the colors of the sunrise. The broad canopy of blue was flawless with neither clouds nor wind driven dust. Tate looked at Maggie as she sat hugging her knees and marveled at the slightly curly red hair that rested on her shoulders and hid her face from him. He had become accustomed to her presence and felt incomplete without her near. Even his time of prayer was often interrupted with images of the woman, especially when he thought about the possibility of their time together coming to an end. They had, after all, completed the purpose of their journey. Now that she was reunited with her father, what would she do and what should he do?

"Your father's doing well, isn't he?" asked Tate.

"Yes, even though it's been more'n a week, he is doing very well. Little Otter has had him up and walking several times now." She thought about it a moment, then asked, "Have you noticed anything about the two of them?" She turned and looked back at the semi-reclining Tate, watched as he lay back with hands under his head, and smiling, lay back beside him, also clasping her hands behind her head as a pillow.

"Whaddya mean?" asked Tate, curious.

"She never leaves him, except to go outside and fix him something to eat. They're always talking and yesterday, when I went in the tipi, they were talking but stopped when I came in, they even looked guilty!"

Chuckling, Tate answered, "Maybe they were talking about things that children shouldn't hear!"

Maggie sat up to lean on one elbow and looked at Tate grinning. She playfully smacked his chest, "Children? Just cause he's me father, doesn't make me a child!"

"Well, maybe they've got some special friendship developing. After all, she doesn't have a man and your mum's gone to glory, so, why not?"

Maggie's brow furrowed, then with a pensive expression painting her face, she lay back to think about what her friend just said. "You don't really think . . . "

"Why not? Might be just what they both need," answered Tate, chuckling.

"But what about me? I just found me father and now . . . "

"Now what? He's still your father and you're still his daughter, right?"

"Well, yeah, but . . . "

"I've been meanin' to talk to you about that," drawled Tate, seriously but smiling.

"About what?" asked an exasperated redhead. She wasn't used to being interrupted so many times in one conversation.

"About what you want to do. Are you thinkin' about going back to the city?"

"I really hadn't thought much about it. I've just been focused on finding me father, and not looking at anything else." She sat up and turned to face Tate, "I do know that going back to the city is not what I want to do, after being in the mountains and seeing this beautiful country, how could anyone go back to the crowded dirty city?"

"That still doesn't answer the question, what do you want to do?" asked Tate as he sat up to face the woman.

"Oh, I dunno. Any ideas?" she asked coyly, letting a smile slowly cross her face.

"Matter o' fact, yeah. See, I built me a cabin down south of here in the Sangre de Cristo mountains, and I was thinkin' 'bout headin' that way, maybe spendin' the winter there. How would you like to come along?" asked Tate, trying to appear nonchalant. He reached down and plucked a piece of foxtail grass, put the stem in his mouth and looked to Maggie for her response.

She stared at him and her brow slowly furrowed as she asked, "Just what do you mean, 'come along'?"

"Well, like we been doin', ya' know, travelin' together. Ya' don't have no home anywhere an' my cabin's empty, an' well . . ." he tried to remain somber but failed as a smile tugged at the corners of his mouth.

Maggie squinted and wrinkled her nose as she asked, "Are you asking me . . ."

He could contain it no longer and started laughing out loud as he put his hands at the sides of her shoulders to hold her as he replied, "Yup, guess I am." He pulled her to him and wrapped his arms around her as she put hers around his neck and they shared a long, lingering kiss that broke with both of them laughing.

They stood for a few moments, Maggie resting her forehead on Tate's chest and both of them clasping hands at their sides. Maggie lifted her eyes to Tate to see him smiling down at her and she smiled and stretched on tiptoes for another kiss. Then hand in hand, they started down the slope of the hill toward the village, each with many thoughts swirling in their minds.

"Uh, since there is no church or parson or anyone like that around, what are we going to do?" asked Maggie.

"I'm thinkin' we could have a Ute ceremony, it seems to work for them and like you said, there's not anyone else. Whaddya think?" inquired Tate.

"What do they do?"

"Well, each tribe and band have different practices, I guess we could talk to Singing Bird and White Buffalo Horn, maybe work out some form of compromise. I think what's important is that God knows our hearts and it won't be so much the words or ceremony as the intent and purpose. And of course, I'll be needin' to talk to your father," added Tate.

Maggie looked up at her man and said, "I think me father already knew."

"What?"

"He caught on the first day and told me I was in love with you."

Tate stopped and turned her to him and said, "Why didn't you say something?"

"Well, I wasn't sure how you felt and, well, I was afraid of what you'd say. But not anymore," she said as she leaned against him playfully. "So, when are we going to do this?"

"Are you in a hurry?" he asked.

"Well . . . " she started before he interrupted.

"I think we'll have to wait until your father's able to be there, course that shouldn't be too long. And unless I miss my guess, I imagine Little Otter and Singing Bird will have something to do with it. You see, with most native people, it's a pretty special thing when a couple go through the joining ceremony. Not so much different than white people, you know, fancy dress, feastin' and such. But, shouldn't take too long. 'Sides, I'd like to see us get to the cabin with time to stock up for the winter and such."

When they returned to the lodge, Daniel was sitting outside, leaning against a willow backrest, feet toward the cooking fire and Little Otter was busy with a pot of stew suspended over the flames. As the two approached, holding hands, Daniel let a broad smile part his whiskers and said, "So, you two finally decided to do it, eh?"

Maggie looked exasperated and said, "What do you mean?"

"Well, from the looks of you two, I'd be guessin' you're ready to get hitched!"

As they talked, Little Otter went to the side of the big Irishman, knelt by his side and rested her hand on his shoulder. Maggie looked at Tate to see if he noticed and turned back to her father. She started to speak but was stopped by Tate's touch to her arm.

"I meant to talk to you first, sir. I would need your permission, of course," stated Tate, "but I would like to marry your daughter, if that would be acceptable to you."

The big Irishman let loose with loud laughter that shook his rotund girth, and answered, "Why, Laddie, of course you have me permission. I'd be happy to see the two of you married."

Both Daniel and Little Otter smiled broadly at the news and with a quick smile to Daniel, Little Otter stood and returned to her duties at the cook fire. She looked at Maggie and said, "I am happy for you. Have you told Singing Bird?"

"No, but we'll go there right away. We also want to talk to White Buffalo Horn about the ceremony, and I'd like to talk to you as well. There is much I need to know. Will you help me? You know, my mother is gone, and I have no one."

Little Otter smiled and said, "I would be honored. Do you want me to serve as one to stand in for your mother?"

Maggie smiled, nodding her head, "Yes, yes, I would. That would be wonderful."

"It will be an honor for me. There will be much to do and Singing Bird will want to be a part as well," remarked Little Otter, busy at her task. She looked to Daniel, smiled and back at Maggie. "Morning Sky has made her father happy."

"It is good that you will be joined. I am pleased that you will do this as part of our people." The words of Lame Buffalo were translated by Little Otter for Tate and Maggie, seated in the lodge of the chief. "My woman will help Otter and Bird to prepare you," nodding to Maggie, "for the joining." He looked to Tate, "Have you prepared for the feast?"

Tate was surprised at the question, "I do not understand."

"There will be a feast of celebration before the joining. It is your duty to provide the meat for that feast for the village." Lame Buffalo looked at Tate and began to smile, knowing the man was surprised at this responsibility. "It is good for you that our warriors are preparing for a hunt of the buffalo. There is a herd moving beyond the ridge," motioning with his chin to the long eastern ridge that split the park, "and you will be welcome to join. It will take two buffalo for the village to feast at your joining." The somber leader watched the reaction of the white man and slowly grinned as he saw Tate relax.

"It would be an honor for me to join the hunt. It is also an honor to provide for the feast. I am certain I will bring down at least two buffalo." Tate was seated cross-legged across from Lame Buffalo and looked at Maggie and Lame Buffalo.

"The buffalo cannot be taken with the white man's rifle, it must be taken as a tribute to the Great Spirit and with the bow or the lance," instructed the chief, somberly.

"That is good. I will take the buffalo with my bow as I have done before," answered Tate, pleased at the opportunity to use his longbow.

The chief showed surprise that this white man had taken a buffalo with a bow and asked, "You have done this before?"

"Yes, Lame Buffalo, that is why I am called Longbow. I hunted with the Kiowa and chief Dohäsan gave me the name Longbow. It will be an honor to once again hunt with a great people."

AT FIRST LIGHT the following morning as Tate returned from the mountain and his time of prayer, he was greeted by two warriors by the lodge.

"I am Bear Chaser," said the first man, tapping on his chest, then with a motion to the other, "He is Dull Knife. Lame Buffalo said we are to be with you during the hunt. We will go soon, you must get your horse and weapons and we will return."

As the introductions were made, the men clasped forearms in greeting and as the two prepared to leave, Tate replied, "I will be ready upon your return." He stepped into the tipi to tell the others and saw they were busy with readying their own things. "Are you coming too?" asked Tate, looking at Daniel as he slipped the repaired buckskin tunic over his head.

"Aye, laddie, but I'll not be riding in the hunt. I think I'll find me a place to sit, an' if I get a chance, I'll put me rifle to the task. It's a good 'un, and I'm certain Little Otter would be glad for the meat," he answered, nodding to Otter who smiled at his comment.

"And you're coming too?" he asked of Maggie.

"Well, Otter tells me the women follow the men and work at the butchering. It seems the hunt takes all the people. Even the children help," replied the redhead.

Tate knew what the hunt involved. He had seen other Indian villages on a buffalo hunt and knew the women and even the children were largely responsible for the skinning and butchering of the animals and he also knew that Maggie had no idea what the day would bring. He looked from Maggie to Otter and back again and said, "Alright, but just be ready for a very different day than you've ever seen before."

Tate brought the horses to the lodge and began saddling and gearing the animals with Maggie and Daniel helping. Otter had saved the travois and now brought it to the horses and said, "This will be used to haul the meat." Although Tate had planned on using the packs he yielded to Otter's suggestion and rigged the travois to Daniel's packhorse and the four were soon ready. Bear Chaser and Dull Knife rode up, and with stoic expressions, motioned for them to follow.

Red Hawk, the sub-chief given the responsibility for the hunt, gathered the warriors together after they crossed the low end of the long ridge. He began to divide the group into three smaller groups. He directed Bear Chaser, "You will go to the far side of the draw and place your hunters in ambush. Dull Knife, you will place yours on this side. I will take the others and we will drive the herd to you." Without further explanation, Red Hawk reined his mount around and the larger group of about thirty warriors followed.

Tate stood in his stirrups and surveyed the area. There were two ridges that ran somewhat parallel with a wide dry wash in the middle. The ridge they crossed was thickly timbered on the gully side and stretched north for several miles. The other was a serrated ridge with many smaller ridges extending into the dry wash and thinly covered with piñon and juniper. He saw it would be a perfect funnel to bring the buffalo to them and the stampede would be slowed as it neared the boggy flats of the Platte River.

Maggie and Daniel had not been assigned to either group and Tate motioned for them to join his group as they started for the far side of the wide draw. A dry gulch with considerable sage and cactus on the edge, offered excellent shooting positions for the hunters of Bear Chaser's group. The horses were tethered a short distance away amidst a cluster of juniper and the hunters busied themselves preparing their spots. Daniel and Maggie, both with Hawken rifles, found a scattering of flat sandstone and began piling them together for their shared site. Tate helped with the stones, knowing he would be standing to use his longbow and would not utilize any special cover. At most, he would be below the bank of the gulch, but would probably be standing above. When they were situated, Tate gave a cursory look to the other hunters and noted several had trade fusils, a couple had better flintlock rifles, and the others were armed with bows and arrows. He had noted that all those with rifles had been sent with Bear Chaser and Dull Knife while Red Hawk had only those armed with bows and lances. He knew that reloading a rifle while riding alongside a buffalo would not be an easy task, whereas a good warrior could easily send four or five arrows into their quarry in the same time another man could reload once.

It was just a short while before the thunder of the stampeding herd echoed between the ridges and everyone hid themselves. Tate stepped into his bow, stretched the string to the top nock of the stave and had his bow ready. His quiver hung at his waist and he nocked an arrow in readiness.

A billowing dust cloud showed the nearness of the

rumbling mass of dark brown and the thunder of their stampeding hooves seemed to overwhelm the entire dry wash.
They felt the trembling of the ground beneath them and
Maggie's eyes grew wide as she looked from Tate to her
father. The bellowing of the beasts, the clatter of horns, and
the pounding of their hooves drew everyone's attention to
the approaching herd. Excitement rose as the hunters
fidgeted, checking their gear, looking to one another,
watching the brown mass nearing.

Suddenly they were upon them and each warrior tensed
and prepared their shot. The thunder of the herd was
drowned by the roar and blasts of the rifles. Smoke belched
from the muzzles as the screams of the mounted hunters
sounded. Tate stood, stepped into his bow and as he reached
full draw, followed a lumbering bull as he sighted down the
shaft of the arrow and he let it fly. His eyes never left the
arrow as it buried itself in the thick fur of the bull, the
fletching protruding just behind the front leg. As he watched
the bull, he unconsciously nocked another arrow and sent it
after the first. When he saw it strike, he turned his eyes to
another and sent two more arrows into a big cow. He
watched as the cow stumbled and staggered for about fifteen
more yards before dropping her head into the dirt and flipping end over end and landed on her back.

The massive herd continued to thunder past and as Tate
nocked another arrow, he looked to see Maggie reloading
and grinning. Daniel was taking aim, apparently at his
second target and Maggie, finished with reloading, brought
the muzzle down and took aim at another. Tate watched as
she followed her target and squeezed off her shot. The blast
of the Hawken belched smoke and Tate saw a young bull
stagger and fall. He smiled at the woman and rested his hand
on her shoulder.

"Is that two?" he hollered to be heard.

Maggie looked up at him as she started reloading, nodding her head and grinning. He motioned to her that two was enough and to let the others pass. Maggie reached to her father's shoulder and motioned for him to stop. He nodded and sat back. The herd had already dwindled to the stragglers and the bowmen were taking them. The rest of the herd had made a muddy mess of the river bottom at the end of the wide draw, but nothing was going to stop their flight. Tate knew they would soon tire and settle down as the warriors would pursue them no further. He looked at Maggie and Daniel and said, "So, whaddya think of your first buffalo hunt?"

"It was exciting! It's going to take me a couple days just to settle down, I think," replied Maggie as she looked at her father.

"Aye, it was that. I dinna think I could do it, but it was exciting. But now, I be thinkin' the real work begins," he declared as he struggled to his feet and looked to Tate.

As they talked, Tate saw several of the mounted warriors circling one of his kills and he said, "Follow me," as he started for the group of warriors. They were talking and gesturing as they saw Tate and the others approach and Red Hawk looked at the downed buffalo, the fletching of two arrows within a couple of inches of each other and looked up at Tate.

Red Hawk looked at the arrows in Tate's quiver and back at the arrows in the bull and slowly nodded his head. "This was a good kill. But you were not mounted. Where were you?" asked Red Hawk.

Tate turned and pointed to the rock pile, "There, by those rocks. These two," he pointed to Daniel and Maggie, "were behind those rocks and I was beside them." The other warriors looked at one another and at Tate and watched as he lay his bow across the neck of the bull and withdrew his Bowie knife and sliced open the bull from rib cage to scro-

tum. The steam rose as he pulled the entrails out and he cut a
big chunk of liver and slit the bile bladder. He offered the
bloody mass to Red Hawk, who smiled and took it. The
warrior slipped his knife from the scabbard, dipped the end
of the meat in the bile, sunk his teeth in the dark flesh and
cut it off just in front of his nose, letting blood flow down his
chin and onto his chest. The other warriors shouted as Red
Hawk handed the liver back to Tate who duplicated the
warrior's actions to the cheers of the others. He passed the
liver to another and the act was repeated by each one until
the last of the meat came to the last one of the hunters,
Maggie. She looked at the meat in her father's hand, then at
her father's bloody beard, and she held up her hand and
turned away. The warriors laughed, but not in derision as
they respected her courage to say no to a traditionally male
practice.

When Maggie turned away, she saw the many other
villagers as they began to swarm over the downed carcasses.
Little Otter and Singing Bird came to her, leading the pack
horses and laughing with one another. They motioned for
Maggie to join them, which she quickly and happily did as
they started for the second kill of Tate's. Lobo had stayed
behind with Singing Bird and now followed the women to
the task of butchering, willing to do his part and clean up
some of the scraps.

It was a tired bunch of people that dragged back into the
village well after dark. With heavy laden horses, Maggie,
Tate, Daniel, Little Otter and Singing Bird made their way to
the lodge. After they unloaded the horses, Singing Bird bid
them good night and Tate led the horses back to the herd.
The women stacked and covered the meat, knowing the
work of smoking and drying the meat would begin at first
light. The night passed quickly, and daylight came all too

soon, but there was much to do, and all rolled from their blankets ready to begin.

The village was filled with racks covered with thin sliced meat hanging over slow smoking fires and the villagers were busy with the preparations for the feast. It was always customary to have a large feast after any successful hunt and now with a joining ceremony that also called for a feast; it was a joyous time for everyone. There was music from flutes, cymbals, and drums and dancing to the chants and drums. It was as festive a time as Maggie or Daniel had seen and Tate especially enjoyed watching his wife-to-be as she tried to dance with the others. It was another tiring night and the blankets beckoned to the tired foursome.

CHAPTER THIRTY-FIVE
CEREMONY

First light, the morning of the fourth day after the big feast, and Tate sat alone on the shoulder of the round top mountain, watching the sun paint the eastern sky. It was a special time in prayer with his Lord this morning and his smile spread almost as wide as the colors in the sky. God had taken away all his doubts and filled him with anticipation of the days and years ahead. Today was the day of the joining ceremony and tomorrow they would leave for the cabin in the Sangre's. He stood, stretched wide his arms and tried to absorb the beauty of the sun's first peek over the horizon. He patted Lobo on the head, ran his fingers through the scruff of his neck, and started back down the mountain.

Daniel was by the cookfire, saw Tate coming, and bent down to pour the younger man a fresh cup of coffee. He handed the steaming brew to Tate and sat back down, "So, today's the big day, huh?"

"Yessir, it is. But, I've been meanin' to ask you, what're your plans?" asked Tate as he sat down on the smooth grey log.

Daniel had taken his usual seat with the woven willow

backrest and looked up at Tate and answered, "I ain't rightly sure, laddie. I know there's gold back yonder, but now that my wife's gone, and Margarite leavin' soon, I don't know what I'd do with a pot full o' gold. Seein' as how I'm not a Leprechaun, you know." He chuckled as he pictured himself as the legendary sprite dressed in green and playing tricks on others. "Although, it might be fun to try!"

"I've been noticin' a special friendship between you'n Little Otter. You thinkin' 'bout spendin' a little time with her?" queried Tate, mischievously.

"Well," and he squirmed and moaned a little, grabbing at his wound, "ya know, I dinna heal up as fast as I used to when I was a young pup, an' I'm thinkin' I need a bit more nursin'. Wouldn't you agree?"

Tate chuckled and said, "I guess a wounded man can use all the nursin' he can get."

"Aye, aye, my sentiments, exactly." Daniel scrounged around in his pocket and withdrew his white briar pipe, stuffed it with tobacco, and lit it with a firebrand. He leaned back as he exhaled a puff of white smoke and added, "This is a pretty good life an' Little Otter's a mighty fine woman, she is indeed."

Since the day after the big feast, the women had been conspicuously absent from the lodge, leaving the men to fend for themselves. Daniel had shown himself to be a pretty good cook but willingly yielded to Tate whenever he showed a hankering to do the deed. A young boy had brought them the message about the ceremony the night before and the men now waited for any other word or instructions they were to follow. They had just finished their second cup of coffee when the same young man came to their fire, "You will come with me." Tate looked at the boy, sat his cup down, and stood to follow. Daniel had not moved, but the boy motioned to

Daniel as well and both men followed the youngster through the village.

Just beyond the lodge of Lame Buffalo, was a sizable sweat lodge, smoke rising from the rear, and standing of either side of the entry, were Lame Buffalo and White Buffalo Horn. When Tate and Daniel neared, the Shaman instructed them to disrobe and don the provided breech cloths. When ready, they followed Lame Buffalo into the sweat lodge and seated themselves as White Buffalo Horn entered. When the entry flap was dropped, Lame Buffalo splashed a gourd full of water on the hot rocks at the back end of the lodge and steam filled the small room. Daniel looked to see the sweat lodge was made with a frame of bent willow sticks tied together and covered with hides. It was only by the glow of the coals of the fire that he could make out the structure that arched over his head, allowing only enough room for the men to sit cross-legged, facing one another with their knees just inches apart and their heads almost touching the arched roof.

White Buffalo Horn began with a chant as he shook a gourd rattle and after a few moments, he stopped and began his instructions about married life. After considerable coaching in the ways of the union between man and woman and each one's responsibilities, White Buffalo Horn resumed his chanting. All the while Lame Buffalo kept the steam coming. Each man was dripping with perspiration, repeatedly wiping the running sweat from their forehead to keep it from their eyes, as they labored to breathe. Finally, White Buffalo Horn rose and bent over at the waist to exit the lodge. Lame Buffalo motioned for Tate and Daniel to follow. When they stood, each man breathed deep of the fresh air, but the Shaman motioned for them to follow. They went straight to the stream and waded into the depth of the back-water pool, and hurriedly rinsed off in the frigid water.

As they came from the water, four boys were waiting with bundles for each man. As Tate opened his, he found a new set of buckskins, but these were white with a thin line of blue beading over the crest of each shoulder and across the chest. He was fascinated with the craftsmanship, the stitching was miniscule, almost invisible and each piece of fringe was exactly the same size. When he donned the outfit, it fit him perfectly. He sat down and slipped on the matching set of moccasins and stood, looking down at his new attire.

"Well, laddie. You make quite a sight!" said Daniel. Tate had been so absorbed in his own attire he had neglected the others and lifted his eyes to see Daniel arrayed in a similar outfit. Tate's jaw dropped as he looked at the big man that he thought resembled a cloud and was taken by the look of the white buckskins, similar to his but minus the beading, and the bushy red beard that blossomed across his chest and the red and green Tam O'Shanter that topped it off.

Tate let a broad smile cross his face and said, "Ain't we a pair?!"

Daniel laughed and nodding his head in a way that made his beard bounce, "Aye, that we are."

Lame Buffalo, now in a new set of leggings and with his bone and bead breastplate covering his chest, his full eagle feather headdress, motioned for them to follow White Buffalo Horn. The Shaman was arrayed similar to Lame Buffalo but had a headdress of the crown of a white buffalo complete with horns and a cape of the buffalo draping down his neck and back. Both men were impressive in their attire and demeanor. When they came to Lame Buffalo's lodge, there were several blankets lying on the ground and a ceremonial redstone pipe waited in the middle.

Lame Buffalo motioned for the men to be seated, directly opposite one another and Lame Buffalo and White Buffalo Horn seated themselves opposite one another. The four men faced the center of the circle as Lame Buffalo picked up the ceremonial pipe, leaned back to accept the firebrand from White Stone Woman, drew deep to light the tobacco, then rested the pipe on his crossed legs as White Buffalo Horn began a prayer to the Creator. When he finished, Lame Buffalo lifted the pipe to the four directions, then to the sky and to the earth, and putting it to his mouth, he drew deeply and exhaled as he passed the pipe to Daniel. Each man repeated the movements of the chief and the pipe was soon returned to the center of the blankets. Tate nodded to a young man he had waiting, and the young man went beside the lodge and brought out a rifle and the accouterments, handed it to Tate who presented it to Lame Buffalo. "You have honored me by allowing me to be a part of your people. This is to show my thanks." It was the rifle, a good Kentucky style percussion rifle, taken from the attacker, B.O. The young man brought another rifle, which had been taken from Dingus, and Tate presented it to White Buffalo Horn. "For your guidance and help for our joining." Both men admired their gifts, smiling and nodding in appreciation. "It is the custom of many tribes for the man of the joining to give gifts to the leaders of the people when they are joined. It is my honor to keep this tradition with these gifts to you."

"We are also honored to have you as a part of our people, and these gifts will keep you in our memories for many seasons," answered Lame Buffalo.

White Buffalo Horn added, "You honor us with your gifts and we are grateful. But now, it is time." He stood and motioned for the others to stand as well. He motioned them to come alongside and face away from the lodge toward the center of the village. As they did, a flute began playing and a soft drumbeat rose. The flap on the far lodge was thrown back and the first thing Tate saw was the red hair. He smiled as Maggie stood and the white buckskin dress accented the red hair and the broad smile showed her brilliant white teeth and her green eyes sparkled. Her dress was a beautiful creation that many women of the village had carefully prepared for this day. Adorned with designs of blue and white beads, accented by small tin bells, white ivory elk's teeth and porcupine quills and carved wing bones from eagles. Tufts of fur decorated the tips of the long flowing fringe that dangled from her arms and across her chest and back. It was a beautiful creation, but Tate was focused on the freckled face and sparkling eyes.

Maggie had taken no more than three steps from the lodge when another woman, also in white, stepped through the entry. When she stood, her dress as beautiful as Maggie's, Tate recognized Little Otter, smiling broadly and looking directly at Daniel. Tate looked to the big man, back at Little Otter, then to Maggie, and realized what was happening. This wasn't just the joining of Maggie and Tate, it was also for Daniel and Little Otter. He turned to look at the big grinning Irishman and chuckled at the man, "You really are a Leprechaun!" he declared.

The joining ceremony was simple with a prayer to the Creator by the Shaman, a joining of hands by the couples and a binding of wrists together by the chief. At the conclusion, Lame Buffalo lifted the joined hands of the two couples high and announced, "The two are now one!" The villagers burst out in cheers and the drums began to signal the beginning of the celebratory dance. But the couples were sent away to the lodges prepared for each couple. They were not to be seen until the next morning.

GOODBYES ARE NEVER EASY. IN A LAND AND TIME THAT IS
fraught with danger from man, beast and nature alike, there
are no promises of tomorrows. The big Irishman enveloped
his little redhead in his arms holding her tight pillowing her
head on his beard. Maggie leaned back with tear-filled eyes,
stood on tiptoes and gave her father a quick kiss and turned
away to run to her pinto and mount up. She dabbed at her
eyes, forced a smile and instructed Little Otter, "You take
care of that man, you know he needs you to keep him out of
trouble."

Little Otter smiled, nodding her head, "And you take care
of that man. He needs you just as much as your father
needs me."

Maggie smiled back and nodded her head in agreement.
The women had conspired together to get the men to agree
to meet in the spring. But both women knew it would be a
long and probably hard winter before the green up beckoned. Singing Bird stood beside her grandparents as they
watched the newlyweds ride from their village. Tate and

Maggie twisted around in their saddles to wave again to their friends, then dropped back in their seats to look to their trail. It would be a long ride, Tate estimated it to be ten days to two weeks, before they would get to the cabin, and summer was quickly fading.

The first three days travel was over familiar country, taking the same route they traversed from the Sawatch mountains into the Bayou Salado. Without the need for exploring every valley as they did during their search for Daniel, their journey was easy as they stayed in the flats or near the tree-line. Weather was pleasant and the two enjoyed one another's company as they willingly shared more of their lives.

It was the beginning of the fourth day when Tate pointed their horses to the notch between the end of the Sawatch Range and the beginning of the Sangre de Cristo range. They followed an old Ute Indian trail that had been used for centuries, even to the time of the explorations of the Spanish Conquistadors. When they broke from the aspen at the crest of Poncha Pass, so called by the Utes meaning a foot path, Tate reined up and sat still to both enjoy and appreciate Maggie's response to the view of the San Luis Valley and the long line of granite topped peaks that marched away to the south east.

She stood in her stirrups and stared, then slipped from her saddle to stand on a slight mound and shading her eyes, she looked at the vast valley before her. To her left, the Sangre de Cristo range lined out with the grey peaks stretching to the blue sky as if reaching for heavenly treasure. The dark blue timber skirts fell from the mountains shoulders and flared to the valley as the ragged edge of those skirts taunted the streams and grass below. To her right, smaller timber covered mounds spread out as a welcome mat stretching to distant mountains barely seen to the far south-west. The valley was marked by streams along the east, some coming from the west, and an assortment of muted colors across the undulating flats that told of sage, rabbit brush, oak brush, cacti, and buffalo grass. Away to the south, a few clouds hung around the edge of the clear blue sky like pearls from the neck of a queen.

Maggie stood breathless, then suddenly whirled to face Tate asking, "Is this home?" with eyes wide in expectancy and hope.

Tate let a smile paint his face as he leaned on the pommel of his saddle, arms crossed, and nodded, "Yup. Our cabin is way down there," pointing to the retreating Sangre's, "sittin' back in those trees on the side of those mountains."

"Oh, Tate! It's beautiful! I can't wait to see our home, I know I'm going to love it! This whole valley is wonderful!" she declared as she twirled back around like a ballerina, arms swinging wide. She stopped and looked again and turned back to Tate smiling broadly. "Thank you, my husband!" as she dropped her eyes in a coy smile.

"Well, come on, let's move back into them trees a bit, have ourselves a bite to eat and give these horses some rest, what say?" He reined his horse around to lead the way to the cove of aspen and grass that beckoned.

As they sat on the grass, munching on the cornbread and smoked buffalo, Maggie asked, "Are there Indians here?"

Tate grinned, "Maggie, there's Indians everywhere in this country. But hereabouts, well," he pointed to the nearby mountains to their right along the western edge of the valley, "This here's Caputa Ute territory. Now further south there, that gets into Mouache Ute territory. Along the southern edge of the valley, well, that's Jicarilla Apache, and to the east o' them, that's Comanche country."

"What about these mountains?" asked Maggie, pointing to the Sangres.

"Well, just about all of 'em hunt in those mountains, but they prefer to live in these hills to the west. Winter ain't so bad on this side, mountains ain't as high and they don't get as much snow," explained Tate.

"Are they friendly?" queried the girl.

"Most of 'em, 'ceptin' the Apache, they can be a little cantankerous."

Tate motioned for Lobo to scout ahead and the caravan of four horses and two riders took the trail to the east of the spring fed creek. Daniel had added to their supplies with his bounty from the attackers and his trip to the trader and Tate had commandeered the extra horse taken from B.O. to use as a second packhorse. Daniel knew he would fare well living with the Yamparika and wouldn't make a trip to the traders until spring when they were to meet at Bent's fort.

Their second night along the Sangre de Cristo saw them with fresh meat from a lone doe mule deer taken at dusk. Their camp was back in the trees and unseen from the valley floor and Tate was confident their fire wouldn't be seen from below. The steaks sizzled over the fire as the coffee perked on the rock beside the flames and Maggie tended the fresh vegetable mix in the frying pan. Lobo lay with his head between his paws, staring at the dripping steaks. Tate froze when Lobo's ears perked, and the wolf rose quickly to his feet, staring and growling at the lower edge of the trees. The horses also turned, heads up, ears pricked looking below. Tate reached for his rifle, Maggie saw him move and his concerned look and slowly walked to where her rifle stood leaning against a tree. Tate slowly stood, stepped back toward a tree, and called out, "Come in if you're friendly, if not, you might wanna settle accounts with your maker, cuz you're about to meet him."

Soundlessly, three Ute warriors stepped from the trees into the light of the fire. The leader held a rifle down by his side, while the other two had arrows nocked in their bows but kept them pointed down. The leader slowly walked forward, looking at Tate with a slight scowl. Tate thought the man looked familiar, but he didn't want to lower his rifle to use sign language, "You are welcome, and we will share our food with you," nodding toward the fire. The leader furrowed his brow, showing his lack of understanding. Maggie translated into Ute the words of Tate, surprising both Tate and the Leader. The leader looked at the woman, standing back in the shadows, and asked their names.

"He is called Longbow, and I am Morning Sky and he," pointing at Lobo, "is Lobo. We go to our cabin in the mountains."

Although all the men were surprised and somewhat apprehensive to see the wolf, their attention turned to the redhead translator. The leader showed recognition at the name Longbow, looked at Tate, and began to grin. "Longbow, I am Two Eagles. We met in this valley, long ago. You were with a black man."

When Maggie translated, Tate lowered his rifle and keeping it cradled under his arm, he signed, "It is good to see an old friend. Join us for our meal."

The time of the meal passed quickly with much conversation. Maggie explained about learning the Ute language from the Yamparika and Two Eagles was impressed with her translating and with her red hair, having never seen anyone with such before. The three men, now better friends than before, left to return to their own camp about a mile away and Tate and Maggie soon turned to their blankets, full and happy.

"OH, I never seen such colors in all my life!" declared Maggie as she turned to look at Tate. They were sitting on the porch of the cabin and watching the sunset paint the heavens with a palette of hues of orange, yellow, gold and red. "The sunset is magnificent, but the colors of all the aspen and oak brush are beyond words to describe. Oh, Tate, it is so beautiful!"

"Yeah, this is my favorite time of year. Seems like even the animals like it best. The elk and deer are matin' up, the bears and others are stockin' up, and we've done our stockin' up. Yup, great time o' the year."

When they arrived at the cabin, Tate was pleased to see that little needed to be done to get everything in fine shape. The corrals needed some repair, some grizzly had carved his mark on the door to the cabin but failed to break in, and everything else was fine. They spent most of the past several weeks stocking their larder. After smoking most of the meat, they stored it in the cool of the cavern behind the cabin. Maggie had learned about tanning hides from Little Otter and put that knowledge to use, providing them with warm robes for the winter. And now they were enjoying a short respite from their labors.

Maggie leaned on the rail and scanned the valley as the colors from the sunset painted the prairie, and nonchalantly said, "This will be a great place to raise a family."

Tate slowly let a frown mark his forehead and he stood to stand beside his wife. He looked down at her, trying to see if she was hiding something. She glanced up at him and asked, "Don't you think so, Mr. Saint?" as she rocked back and forth against the rail, turning her head slightly away from him.

"Well, yes I do. Of course, I do, but what got you to thinkin' about that?"

She let go of the rail and started counting on her fingers, "Let's see now, October, November, December, January, February, March, April, May, June. Yup, that's about right."

She turned and grinned at Tate, who finally realized what she was saying. A big smile spread across his face as he wrapped his arms around her waist and picked her off the floor of the porch and stretched his arms to lift her high. He kissed her long and hard and said, "Yup, it's a great place to raise a family!"

A LOOK AT PATHFINDER PERIL (ROCKY MOUNTAIN SAINT BOOK 6) BY B.N. RUNDELL

If the man of the mountains, Tate Saint, had a fault, it was that he had a hard time saying no whenever someone needed his help. But now he has a family and the wilderness makes many demands on anyone that tries to master the mountains. And if a redheaded Irish wife, a curios toddler for a son, a wolf for a hunting companion and a bear cub for a playmate for his son wasn't enough, a legendary mountain man, Old Bill Williams, recruits him to help John C. Fremont on his expedition to find a route through the Sangre de Cristo and San Juan mountains in the middle of winter. When the elder statesman of the mountains, Williams, tells Fremont it can't be done, the Pathfinder expects Tate Saint to get them through.

But this venture soon becomes one of the most treacherous and deadly expeditions of the times. Facing the full onslaught of a Rocky Mountain winter with twenty-foot snowdrifts, below zero temperatures, and every other hazard that could be brought to bear, the challenges must be met and conquered. But the things that must be done and the sacrifices that must be made become more than anyone expected or wants to remember. One of the greatest challenges of the young mountain man's life must be met and conquered, or he and many others will die.

AVAILABLE OCTOBER 2018 FROM B.N. RUNDELL AND WOLFPACK PUBLISHING

Born and raised in Colorado into a family of ranchers and cowboys, B.N. Rundell is the youngest of seven sons. Juggling bull riding, skiing, and high school, graduation was a launching pad for a hitch in the Army Paratroopers. After the army, he finished his college education in Springfield, MO, and together with his wife and growing family, entered the ministry as a Baptist preacher.

Together, B.N. and Dawn raised four girls that are now married and have made them proud grandparents. With many years as a successful pastor and educator, he retired from the ministry and followed in the footsteps of his entrepreneurial father and started a successful insurance agency, which is now in the hands of his trusted nephew. He has also been a successful audiobook narrator and has recorded many books for several award-winning authors. Now finally realizing his life-long dream, B.N. has turned his efforts to writing a variety of books, from children's picture books and young adult adventure books, to the historical fiction and western genres.

Made in the USA
San Bernardino, CA
30 July 2020

76264796R00144